D0231186

For David

OXFORD
UNIVERSITY PRESS

Great Clarendon Street, Oxford OX2 6DP
Oxford University Press is a department of the University of Oxford.
It furthers the University's objective of excellence in research, scholarship,
and education by publishing worldwide. Oxford is a registered trade mark
of Oxford University Press in the UK and in certain other countries

Database right Oxford University Press (maker)

First published 2020

British Library Cataloguing in Publication Data

Data available

ISBN: 978-01-9277158-2

1 3 5 7 9 10 8 6 4 2

Printed and bound by CPI Group (UK) Ltd, Croydon, CR0 4YY

Paper used in the production of this book is a natural,
recyclable product made from wood grown in sustainable forests.
The manufacturing process conforms to the environmental
regulations of the country of origin.

The Children of Swallow Fell

Julia Green

OXFORD
UNIVERSITY PRESS

When war came, it came swiftly and suddenly, right into the heart of our lives. It changed everything. It changed me.

How do you begin life all over again?

One

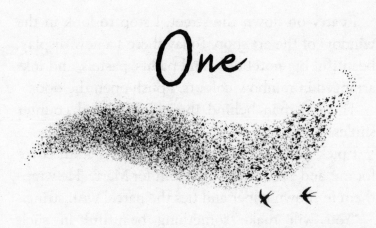

This is how it starts. A Thursday, early March. 4 p.m.

The school bell rings. All day we've been inside, sitting still and doing what we're told. Freedom at last!

Marta and I run out of the schoolyard together.

'Coming back to mine?' I ask.

'Can't, today. I promised I'd be straight home.'

We hug at the corner before she turns off towards the tram station. 'See you tomorrow, Isabella! Call me later. Love you!'

'Love you! *Ciao*!'

For a moment longer I watch Marta, her red bag over her shoulder, the sun on her dark hair. She looks back once, waves, and hurries on to catch the tram home.

I carry on down the street. I stop to look in the window of the art shop. Today there's a new display: beautiful big notebooks and paints, pastels, and inks arranged in rainbow colours. I push open the door.

The old man behind the old-fashioned counter smiles.

I pick out a sketchbook with a green cloth cover for me, and a red one as a present for Marta. He wraps them in brown paper and ties the parcel with string.

'You will make something beautiful in such beautiful books,' he says, 'just like your father. How is he?'

'He's OK,' I say.

He slips a new ink pen into the package and smiles at me. 'A gift, for luck,' he says. 'For the future.'

'*Grazie mille*,' I say. Thank you.

I tuck the parcel into my bag and run on. I dodge the people dawdling along the pavements. I turn down a narrow street, past boarded-up shops, past the high walls of the museum splashed in new red graffiti. A crowd has gathered at the foot of the steps outside the old church. I cross the road and keep running.

I stop for a fruits-of-the-forest *gelato* at the bar on the corner—the best place for ice cream in the whole world. By the time I reach the market square, the stall-holders are already packing up.

Boom!

A massive explosion rocks the city. Silver-grey pigeons take flight from the church roof and wheel skywards. I stare up at the bright blue sky, at the golden cupola of the church, my heart pounding. For a second it's as if everything around me freezes.

And then panic breaks out: everyone's yelling and running, pushing out of the crowded square into the narrow streets in the four corners. The woman packing up the flower stall hisses, '*Hurry home, child!*'

A second explosion blasts out over the city: the sound ricochets off the tall buildings. A series of smaller thuds echo out. The sirens start: police cars, ambulances, fire engines scream their way across the city. There's a strange, bitter smell in the air.

What's happening?

I rush with everyone else, towards the river, towards home and safety. I join the crowd of people waiting impatiently at the road-crossing for the lights to change: cars and vans and buses stream past. Everyone's terrified. *What is it? An accident at the aluminium factory? No, they're bombing the city. A*

bomb at the tram station . . .
My heart misses a beat.
Marta.
My best friend in the whole world.
Marta, close as a sister. Closer, even.
Hurrying to catch her tram home . . .

My phone pings. Two texts. But not from her.

```
Are you OK? Where are you? Come home now!
Dad x
```

```
Just heard—trouble in city centre. You
home yet? Mamma xxx
```

I text back: `I'm fine. Nearly home xxx`

I text Marta. `CALL ME! ?????? xxxxxxxxxx`

The lights change. People rush forward, push and shove across the road and onto the narrow bridge and I'm swept along on the same tide.

I glance back: a plume of smoke rises above the city, ink black. The smoke cloud breaks apart: it's not smoke at all, but hundreds and thousands of birds: the starlings that roost at dusk on the trees and tall buildings near Central Station. They swirl like smoke above the city, over the river, right above me on the bridge. The sky is full of their black wings and panicked voices.

The press of people moves me on over the bridge to the quieter side of the river. I dodge the traffic without waiting for the lights, slip down the narrow cobbled streets towards home. My heart thud thud thuds. Still no message from Marta. *Please let her be all right . . .*

I run past the familiar houses, the small bars and cafés, across the square at Santa Maria, and on again. The swell of people subsides. The smells change too: greener, damper; the familiar cooking smells of tomato and garlic. I'm out of breath, almost home. High above the houses swifts swoop and dive, dark arrows. Their thin screams pierce the air.

I clatter up the steps to our apartment on the third floor. Dad's waiting at the open door.

'At last!' He folds me into his arms. 'Oh, Isabella!' He squashes me to his chest. 'Thank goodness you're OK.' His breath is hot on my head.

He sounds as if he might actually cry.

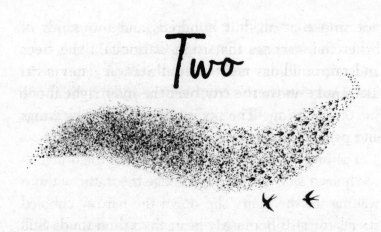

Two

We try to find out what's happening, but there's some kind of news blackout. The internet's down. The telly's showing old black and white films and quiz shows instead of news or current affairs programmes. Dad turns off the TV and retunes the radio to music while he cooks supper: pasta and pecorino and peas. I make a salad with tomatoes and rocket leaves from the fridge. I keep calling Marta to make sure she got home OK, but she doesn't answer. Maybe her phone just isn't working. Or, or . . .

Mum still hasn't come home. She's not answering her phone, either. Dad calls her office but no one picks up. He says he *thinks* she said she had a meeting after work, but he isn't sure what for, or where. He phones my sister, Gabriella. She's been in lectures all day and then at the library and in her flat. Dad says there's trouble here and maybe it will be the same in her university city, too. He makes her promise to stay safe and not go out. He passes the phone to me.

'Is Dad still listening?' she says quietly.

'Yes,' I say.

'There's stuff going on here, too,' she whispers. 'But don't say anything to Dad.'

'He's gone into the kitchen now,' I tell her. 'What kind of stuff?'

'A massive protest in the city centre. Train and bus drivers are on strike. They shut the university library at four and told us to go home.'

I jig anxiously from one foot to the other. What does it all mean?

Gabriella keeps talking. 'But I'm fine. Don't worry about me. Or Mum. I'm sure she'll call when she can.'

I start telling her about Marta.

A door slams in her flat. Someone shouts out her name.

'Got to go. Love you.'

And that's it. The phone purrs in my ear. She's gone.

We eat supper, and clean the dishes, and sit out on the verandah to watch the swifts, and all the time, Dad's shaking. His hand trembles when he lifts his glass; his knee rattles the table.

Ambulance and fire engine sirens wail across the city. More explosions boom out in the distance. There's a bitter smell in the air like burning plastic.

'Bombs,' Dad says.

'But why?'

'They'll be targeting historic monuments, transport hubs, bridges. Wiping out the past.'

'*Who* will?'

Dad doesn't answer.

How can this be happening here, to us?

'I can't get through to Marta,' I say. 'She was on her way home. By tram.'

Dad shakes his head.

'Where did Mum say she was going?' I ask him, again.

'I can't remember. I assumed it was a work

meeting, but maybe she said something else, I wasn't paying attention.'

On any other day it wouldn't matter, but this day it does. He looks terrible.

'It'll be OK,' I tell him. 'She'll be home soon. I guess the trams and buses aren't working and it's too far to walk, so she's stayed over with someone. Don't worry.'

It's me, comforting Dad. Even then, I know that's the wrong way round.

But that's the way it goes, from then on, as if we swapped places that night, Dad and me, and now I have to be the grown-up.

Mum's still not back by my bedtime. I have a shower, get into bed, and lie on top of the sheet in the dark. I try calling Marta for the millionth time: still nothing. I try her mum's number, and Ilaria and Giancarlo from school, but there's no connection. I can't get through to anyone. The internet's still not working.

The flat is hot and stuffy. Dad moves around the kitchen putting stuff away, opens the fridge, pours another drink, switches on the radio and turns it down low, so I can only just hear the music. It stops for some kind of announcement: a news bulletin? I stay in bed, not wanting to know. If it's something bad, I don't want to hear it, not yet. It's as if I need to stay ordinary me, nearly-thirteen-year-old Isabella— for one last night.

Three

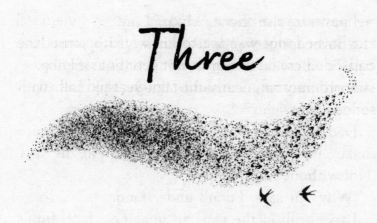

The house phone rings early morning; it's only just getting light. The ringing persists, loud and urgent, and Dad can't have heard it so I run to pick up before it stops. I'm breathless. 'Hello?'

'Isabella! You're OK?' Mum's voice, faint.

'Yes! Are you? What happened? Where are you? Mamma?'

There's a hissing sound, then silence, then her voice again, fainter. 'Get Dad for me, please. There's not much time.'

He's already stumbling bleary-eyed from the front bedroom, his feet flapping in slippers along the hallway.

I pass him the phone. 'Mum,' I say.

I hover to listen. I notice his frayed pyjamas, the creases where he's been sleeping, or not sleeping.

Early morning sunshine floods the hall with sudden light.

Dad turns so I can't see his face, but his voice shakes, his words fracture and break. 'No,' he says. 'Not without you.'

'Why?' he says. 'I don't understand.'

I try to fill in the gaps, to imagine what Mum's telling him. It's unbearable not knowing.

'Tell me what's happening! Where is she?' I say.

Dad's crying. He passes me the phone.

'Mamma? What's going on?'

The line crackles and hums. 'Listen carefully, my lovely girl. Pack up some clothes, some food, essentials only, one bag each you can carry easily. Get yourselves to the Central Station as soon as you can. You'll have to walk. There are no buses or trams. The roads are blocked. Some of the bridges are down. There'll be one last train leaving the city this afternoon, and you two must be on it.'

'Why? Where to? What about you?'

'I'll come later, as soon as I can. I've explained it

all to Dad. I need to collect Gabriella first. You two have to go now. It isn't safe to stay. It's all going to get much worse.'

'I haven't heard from Marta,' I tell her. 'How can I leave when I don't know she's safe? How will you and Gabriella come if there's no more trains?'

'We'll work something out,' she says. 'Now, go and get ready. I want you to leave with Dad as soon as you can. Be strong. I love you.'

So here we are.

The train creaks and sways as it picks up speed. I settle back on the prickly red fabric seat. A woman and two small children and a baby stare back at me from the seat opposite. 'Sshsh,' the woman tells the baby when it cries. She rocks it in her arms until it stops whimpering and falls into snuffly sleep. The little boy shuffles closer to his mother and older sister. The girl hugs her toy rabbit tight.

'We're lucky to find a seat,' Dad says. 'Lucky to get a train before they close the route entirely.' He's still out of breath.

We packed our bags and ran practically the whole way from home. Sounds of explosions echoed over the river. People scurried along like us with bags and bundles and crying babies. Overnight our city had turned into somewhere else entirely. A war zone.

I know a bit about the war, of course. It's been rumbling on for years. It breaks out in different places at different times: *flashpoints*, Mum calls them. It started with the crackdowns on immigration, after the droughts in the south. Climate emergency. Food shortages. Prices shot up. People lost their jobs. Banks closed. Strikes. Protests. Violence, bombs . . . People get arrested. Tanks appear on the streets. The police and army move in. More violence. They show it on the TV news sometimes.

It's always happened *elsewhere*. Other countries. Other cities.

Not *here*. Not *our* city.

This was the last train to leave Central Station. It's some ancient engine they got out of the shed for one last journey, because it runs on diesel fuel instead of electric. The overhead wires are all down. Individual compartments with sliding doors open onto a narrow corridor that runs the length of the train. It smells stale and old. It's packed with people fleeing the city.

I shift my head away from the stained fabric. Once, each seat would have had its own clean cotton pillow.

It's as if we're travelling backwards in time.

Dad bundles our bags onto the old-fashioned rack made of string webbing. He glances at the little family opposite and slumps down next to me. 'Thank goodness we have somewhere safe to go.'

But how does he know? He's not been back to England for years. Is anywhere safe, really? And we've left Mum and Gabriella and Marta and all our friends behind.

Mum sounded so odd, the way she talked.

Be safe. Be strong, she said.

And I am strong.

It's Dad who's crumbling.

After Mum's phone call he sat with his head in his hands, while I packed us a bag each as if we were going on a day trip, not travelling to another country. Clothes, Dad's art things, a book each, my new notebook and pen, food for the journey. At the very last minute I unpinned my favourite photo of Marta and me from my bedroom wall. *Ti amo*, I whispered to her. *Love you*. I tucked the photo inside my notebook to keep it safe.

Dad locked the door of the flat and we ran. The streets were eerily empty without cars or buses or trams. Most of the hurrying people were completely silent. A military helicopter buzzed and circled over the city.

I hand Dad a peach, now, but he shakes his head. 'I'm not hungry.' He tries to pull himself together. 'Thank you, Isabella.'

I offer the boy and the girl a biscuit. The woman nods and smiles at me. They talk in a language I don't understand. The children stare with big round eyes, as if they've already seen too much that's scary.

It's already getting dark outside. The train rattles through empty stations. I peer through the window: I can make out occasional buildings, fields. Distant smoke. We rush through a tunnel and into a deeper kind of dark. The wheels clank along the tracks. Everyone but me falls asleep. Dad leans on me, heavy against my shoulder. I shift to get more comfortable and he rolls the other way.

The train rumbles on through the darkness. Hardly any lights outside. Trees, forest, lakes. I go to find the toilet. The train sways and lurches as I make my way down the corridor. People have pulled down the blinds to most of the other compartments. Perhaps everyone is sleeping now as the train travels through the night.

I can't sleep. My mind spirals with a million questions. Has Mum driven over to get Gabriella yet? Where are they now? What's happening to Marta? Is she safe? Is she leaving the city too, with her mother and grandmother? Where will she go?

And what's wrong with Dad? What's he's not telling me? Is it something to do with Mum?

When I was little, in summer, when it got too hot and dusty in the city, we used to take a slow train up to the hills to Nonna's house. Nonna was Mum's mum, my Italian grandmother. The village houses were painted the colours of the earth: pink and terracotta, umber, yellow ochre and cream. Nonna's house was a deep orange, with green shutters the colour of the olive trees on the terraced hillside behind. We ate our meals outside on the terrace under the shade of the vine. In the evening, the grown-ups stayed at the table, talking and drinking and laughing till long after dark, and I'd fall asleep tucked in close between Nonna and my aunt, Francesca. Often Mum couldn't come, because of her work, and that was just how things were. I didn't pay much attention to all the grown-up talk about politics, back when I was small. But I did hear the urgency in Mum's voice, one time when she was with us at Nonna's.

'*Talking isn't enough, Francesca. We have to actually do something!*'

My aunt stroked my hair. '*But you have responsibilities as a mother, Beatrice.*'

'*What would you know about that? You and Paolo, you've always had money and food and a place to live! You don't care about anyone else.*'

They thought I was asleep. And soon I must have been; I don't remember what happened after that. I guess Dad scooped me up gently and carried me into the house and tucked me into bed, as usual. I loved that little room at Nonna's house, with the simple wooden bed and chair and table, and a china jug and basin for washing your hands and face, and a small square window looking out at hills covered in olive trees. Nonna died two years ago, and the house was sold, and I will never go there ever again.

Now, I think of yesterday's explosions. The news

blackout. What they told us at the station about the overhead wires.

Bombs. Terror. Violence.

Talking isn't enough.

Is my own mother somehow connected with all this?

I reason with myself. My mother is strong and passionate and cares deeply about the world. She stands up against injustice. She writes articles about fairness and inequality. But she'd never do anything violent or destructive. *Books and art and music,* she says. *Beauty, not bombs. Acts of creation, not destruction. That's what the world needs now.*

Four

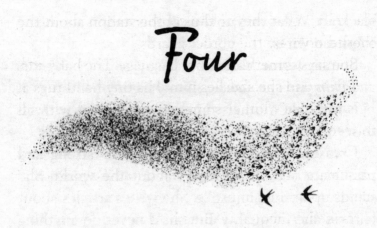

The train creaks to a halt. Doors slam. I must have slept, because someone has pulled down the ancient leather blind over the window. I lift it enough to look out. We're at a station, the first we have stopped at since the journey began, and moonlight shines on jagged mountains. The Alps. Men in uniform line the platform. Some of them climb onto the train.

'The border,' Dad says. He fumbles in his pockets. 'We'll need our papers.'

'They're in the bag, Dad.' I find the papers and passports in the side pocket where I packed them.

The woman opposite wakes, startled. She stares at the guards on the station platform. All down the train, the doors of the compartments are being shoved open by the border guards.

She says something in her language. The baby stirs and frets and she shushes him. His tiny hand tugs at her dress. He's hungry. I look away when she starts to feed him. The other children sleep on.

Our door slides open. A young man in pale grey uniform stands in the doorway. 'Names, passports.' He sounds bored.

'Isabella Alighieri. Daniel Miller.'

'Going to?'

'London. England.'

He scrutinizes the documents.

Why am I nervous, suddenly? There's no reason why we can't travel. England is my father's country. But Dad's anxious, too.

The man hands the passports back. He turns to the woman. She says her name. She fumbles in her bag and produces some folded papers. He smoothes them out, examines them, turns them over.

'No good,' he says. He speaks into his phone. He's reporting the woman and children, calling for backup. A second uniformed man appears. 'Off,' he says. He jerks his thumb to show her what he means.

The woman's terrified. She doesn't understand. The baby cries and the two children wake and stare, silent with terror.

The guards don't help her or explain or anything. 'Hurry. Off the train. No permission to travel in this country.'

'Say something, Dad.' He's got his eyes closed, as if he's asleep. He's pretending that none of this is happening.

I tug his sleeve. 'Dad! We have to help them.'

Dad shakes his head. 'There's nothing we can do,' he mumbles.

The woman pleads with the guards. She holds out the baby, as if to say, *Think of the children . . . this small baby . . . have mercy on this little family . . .*

'Please, let her stay,' I say to the younger guard. 'She's alone with three children. She's no danger to anyone. Think how you would feel if it was you—'

Dad pulls me closer. 'No, Isabella. Shush now.'

'It's not fair. It's not RIGHT!' I blink back tears. 'DO something, Dad!'

But the woman is already gathering her things, strapping the baby to her front, shepherding the children out of the door after the guards. She gives me such a sad, sad smile as she goes through the door into the corridor.

I'm furious with Dad. I move to the opposite seat, pull the blind up further, peer into the darkness. I watch the woman and the children shuffle slowly towards an open door in the station building. The guards are with her, one on each side. The little boy drags his feet, crying, and the younger guard picks him up, swings him onto his shoulders, even though the boy kicks and bites and struggles.

'Don't upset yourself,' Dad says. 'They'll be treated well enough.'

'How do you know? You don't know, and you don't care. If Mamma was here, she'd have done something.'

The train pulls away from the border station. I curl up on the seat. I won't speak to Dad. I watch the shadows thrown by the moonlight, silver and black on the mountains. The train chugs on, steadily climbing, climbing.

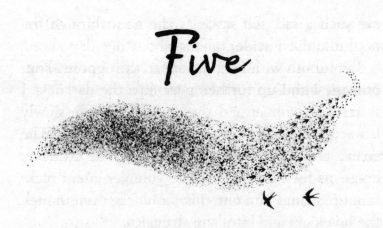

Five

Light creeps into the sky. I lift the blind higher and peer out. Mist hangs low over flat fields; a river meanders through marshy wetlands. A grey heron takes flight, its long legs trailing awkwardly—and then the train's left it all behind and we're rattling through a small grey town. Grey roofs, empty streets. Early morning. We've left the mountains long behind. Dad sleeps on, slumped in the corner of the seat opposite. Quietly, I slide open the carriage door and walk along the corridor to the loo. People in the other compartments are stirring. A woman pours coffee from a flask and the bitter smell makes me suddenly long for this to be a normal morning, me getting ready for school, Mamma making coffee on the kitchen stove, talking about her day ahead at the publishers, asking me what book I'm reading, irritated with Dad for taking too long . . .

The loo stinks.

I splash cold water on my face quickly, rinse my hands, hold my breath till I'm back in the corridor. I stop in the vestibule at the exit doors and pull down the window, gulp in fresh air. The train rattles through a series of small grey towns past boarded-up buildings, graffitied walls. Dogs scavenge along the edge of the railway line. There are a few cars and lorries on the roads, and long convoys of slow-moving military vehicles. A child in a red coat waves from a gate as the train rushes past and I wave back. Is it a normal day for her? Or have the bombs reached her town, too?

And that makes me think of the little family last night. I will never know what happened to them.

I check my phone for the hundredth time. No signal. No messages from Mum, or Marta, or Gabriella, or anyone. In my pocket I find the piece of paper the man at the Termini gave me with the train times in Paris. We will need to queue again for tickets. We might not get on the first train . . . But not everyone will be travelling to England. Most people will stay this side of the European border. Passports and papers are precious. *Like gold dust! Keep them on you at all times*, the man said.

Dad's awake. 'Good morning, Isabella!'

I pull down the bag, check the side pocket, pull out both passports and visas. Phew.

'We should keep these safe on us,' I tell Dad, 'like that man said at the station.' I tuck mine in my pocket and hand the other to Dad.

He nods.

'We're already in France,' I say. 'Not long now. We have to change trains, and cross Paris to another station to find a train through the tunnel. If it's still open.'

I hand him a hunk of bread and cheese. 'That's the last of it.'

Dad does everything so slowly, as if he's in a daze. His hair is all messed up from sleeping. I watch him make his way along the corridor to the toilets, one hand holding the rail to steady himself like an old man. Not like my Dad at all.

We pile off with everyone else at the Gare de

Lyon, Paris. We follow the crowds making their way to the metro station. We work out how to buy tickets, which train to catch for the Gare du Nord. The underground trains are packed, they stink of sweat, people are jammed up against each other. But at least there are trains, and everything still seems to be working, more or less. There are no spare seats. We clutch our bags tight, hemmed in by people with suitcases and backpacks and bags. The train rumbles from station to station, and each time it stops, more people cram themselves on.

'Couldn't we stay here, in Paris?' I ask.

Dad shakes his head. 'And where would we live? We can't afford to pay rent. How would we manage? The city is full of refugees and homeless people sleeping in tents under the bridges, in shop doorways . . . There have been bombs and protests here for a long time.'

'But why?'

'Talking and arguing and voting have got us nowhere. People say direct action is the only way to force change. Bomb the whole lot. It's all a shambles.'

'Do you think that?'

The doors slide open and a group of teenagers

crowd onto the train, hollow-eyed with exhaustion, dishevelled and unwashed.

Dad turns away. 'It's the same everywhere,' he says. 'Corrupt governments. The backlash. And always it's the innocent people who get hurt.'

'I wish we'd stayed. We should have waited for Mamma and Gabriella and all travelled together.'

Dad doesn't answer. He closes his eyes.

I keep checking and re-checking I've got my passport safe. I make Dad do the same. He's still being weird. I have to do everything. When we finally get to the ticket machine at the Gare du Nord, I have to get out actual paper money from a different machine. You can't use a card. There are massive queues for everything. Money, tickets, food, coffee for Dad, water. Our train isn't due for hours.

We wait in the shade of the station like hundreds of other travellers. Dad drinks his coffee. We finish the bread. Finally we clamber onto the crowded train that will take us out of Europe, through the tunnel to England.

At Calais, border guards stop the train to check everyone's passports. Dad goes through his coat pockets: nothing. He stares at me in total panic.

'Check again,' I say. 'Slowly.'

He turns them inside out. Empty. Sweat beads on his forehead. The guards are moving through the train. It will be our carriage next.

'Another pocket?'

Finally he fishes out the crumpled papers and passport from a pocket inside his coat. We breathe out in relief.

The train overheats, there's no air conditioning, the windows don't open. A bunch of thin, scruffy men rush towards the train as if they intend to storm it and climb on. Armed police chase them away.

'Desperate,' Dad mutters. 'Wrong.'

'It's all wrong,' I snap back. 'What would we have done if you'd actually lost your passport just now? No papers. No money. If we'd lost everything?'

He doesn't answer.

The train plunges into the tunnel under the English Channel. All that weight of water pressing down, above us. How is it even safe?

'Not long till London,' Dad says. 'And then just two more trains, to the wild north.'

And so the journey goes on.

A woman sitting opposite tells us there's a slow

train that will take us all the way from London to the north of England. *If you really want to go there!* She shakes her head, as if we're making a mistake.

We have to cross London to another station.

The train's crowded: it's the only one today. *Maybe the last one for a long time*, an old man tells us. *Nothing works in this sad old country any more.*

People on the train look exhausted. Pale. Their clothes are old, worn, grubby. Hardly anyone talks, and when they do, I can't understand the accent. It's a kind of English, but not like Dad and I speak.

The train rumbles on through the edge of the city, past rows of dilapidated brick houses, and then on and on through miles of empty, flat countryside. Fields. Woods. Small towns. The train slows down, stops for ages. *Signals. Broken, as usual*, a man mutters. Eventually the train creaks slowly forward, picks up speed. We rattle through empty stations, past more ruined buildings. There are no lights anywhere. Hardly any cars on the roads, and the ones there are look ancient, rusty. A horse pulls a cart over a river bridge, like something from an old painting. Everything looks run down.

Dad stares out of the window. 'It's all so different,'

he says. 'Not the country it used to be. Not what I remember.'

We both doze. There are hours and hours to go.

A faint *ping* from my phone. A text message. Mum!

`Ti amo, Isabella. I love you. Per`
`sempre. Always.`

I text back: `Love you. Miss you xxxxx`

Nothing happens. The text won't send.

I read her words over and over.

I try to resend my reply, over and over.

I try messaging Marta, and Gabriella, but it's no good. That brief moment of phone signal has gone forever.

Dad shakes me awake. 'Almost there,' he says. 'Next stop.'

We stagger off the train, blinking in the late afternoon light. The platform is deserted. Weeds and wild flowers grow up through the cracked paving stones. The glass roof of the old station building is green with moss. We watch the train disappear up the track.

We stand in the sudden silence and stare at the empty car park, the deserted roads. No street lights. What now?

'Start walking,' Dad says.

'You're joking! How far is it?'

'Thirty-five, maybe forty miles. Someone will pass us. We can hitch a lift.'

'What if they don't?'

But we've not gone far out of the station when we hear a car. Dad sticks his hand out. A battered van slows down, stops. An old man leans out of the window. I hardly understand a word he says, but Dad does. He talks to the man. They seem to argue about something, then the man nods and Dad hands over money.

'Hop in,' Dad says. 'He can take us the whole way.'

The roads are full of potholes and weeds. The man doesn't say much. Dad sits in the front next to him, and I have to crouch in the back next to sacks that smell of earth and animals.

We go through a small deserted town and the man pulls up in front of a scruffy shop and tells Dad to stock up with whatever food he can find. 'There won't be much in the shop, and nowt at all where you're headed,' he says. He stops again to fill the van up with petrol from an ancient pump at a garage at the end of the town. He has to crank the pump by hand. There's an old woman at the petrol station taking the money, but no one else. Where *is* this? Where are all the people?

'There's no electricity any more,' the man tells us. 'Hope you got candles and a lantern up there.'

'There'll be all that, and more,' Dad says. 'From the old days. I lived there as a child.' He says his parents' names, Frieda and Tom Miller, and the man nods slowly, as if he might possibly have heard of them, a long time ago. He mumbles something about *the accident*, and *water*.

The road gets narrower as it climbs up from the valley bottom, and the houses more spaced out. We pass two or three farmhouses, then nothing but hills and fields sloping steeply upwards, and a few trees, and water rushing down the hillsides and along the side of the road. The van splashes through a ford where a stream flows right over the road.

Dad points out the old stone barns in each field, once used for hay and for animals. He looks calmer and happier than he's been the whole journey.

For Dad, this is coming home.

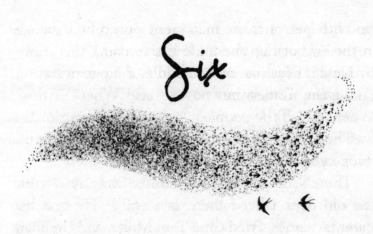

Six

Home.

But this isn't my home.

We've come to the very end of the tarmac road: the rest was washed away. The river regularly floods. *Keep an eye and an ear on her*, the man says, as if the river is a person. We bump down a rough track to the final village, a cluster of grey stone houses huddled under the steep hillside, a disused chapel, a building that might once have been a village hall. There are no lights at any of the windows.

The man doesn't even turn off the engine: he can't wait to get away. Dad lifts out the shopping and our bags, and the man grunts 'good luck' before reversing back up the track to the road.

Now it's just us, in the middle of nowhere.

'Listen,' Dad says.

'What?' All I can hear is the faint whine of the van as it weaves its way back along the road, and a rushing sound. 'There's nothing here!'

'Exactly. But you can hear the river, and wind blowing through grass and heather. Breathe in that pure air! Isn't it beautiful? All this space!' He holds out his arms. 'See how the village nestles under the hill? How safe it feels?'

'Which one is the house? Have you got the key? Dad! Come back!'

He turns and waves towards the bigger house at the far end, set slightly apart from the others. 'The key will be under the loose flagstone by the front door,' he calls. 'That's where they always kept it.'

I lug our bags to the door. It's pitch dark close to the house. I fumble under the stone. Nothing. I turn the iron handle and push against the door but of course it's locked.

Dad expected the house to be waiting for us, door key under the stone, everything as it used to be!

I slide down onto the stone step, rest my head against the door. I'm so tired I could weep. 'Let's break a window,' I say. 'Climb in.'

'No no no. I'll go round the back. The key must be somewhere. They always left a key.'

'Dad, you haven't been back for years. No one has been here for years.'

He crashes round the back, knee-deep in nettles and weeds and a garden gone wild. He swears when he hurts himself on something.

I close my eyes, rest my head on my knees. It goes quiet. In the dark, the river sounds louder.

It begins to rain, softly at first. I open my eyes, watch the drops splash onto the flagstones, patter on the leaves. I shift position closer to the shelter of the house. Something pale and ghostly floats across the garden. A bird. A hunting barn owl on silent wings.

I shiver. This is all so strange. Yesterday we were living our ordinary life in the busy city and now—this!

Nothing. Nowhere. No one.

Dad crashes back through the dripping garden. He holds something up.

'Found the spare! Knew it would be there.'

He turns the key in the lock, the door creaks open, we stumble inside.

The house has been shut up for years. Dust lies thick on every surface. The air smells musty and stale and damp. We go into the front room, pull dust covers off the sofa and chairs. It's so dark we have to prop open the door to let in the last remaining light to see anything at all.

'It's so sad and neglected!' Dad mutters.

'Honestly, Dad! What did you expect?'

He's been imagining the home he lived in as a child, warm and comfortable and loved. But that was a very long time ago.

We're both totally exhausted.

'Let's just camp down here tonight, Dad. We'll sort everything out tomorrow.'

He nods.

I curl up on a squashy old armchair. Dad stretches out on the sofa.

Outside, the rain patters steadily and the river rushes on.

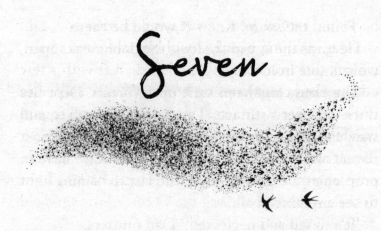

Seven

Early morning. Birdsong. Pale sunlight through the window casts square patterns on a faded green carpet. Dad's snoring, flat on his back on the sofa. It comes to me with a sudden rush where we are: the long journey to get here, the remoteness of the house.

I tiptoe past Dad out into the hall, explore each room downstairs. Everything is shabby and covered in dust. There's an old-fashioned dining room with a tatty wooden table and odd chairs and stained rugs, a small bathroom with a tiled floor and an ancient toilet with an iron cistern and a chain to pull (nothing happens: it doesn't work). The big kitchen at the back has a tiled floor, a chipped enamel sink and wooden draining board, a wobbly table and chairs, a black cast iron cooker. Wooden shelves with a few odd cracked china cups on hooks. There's a separate walk-in larder with a cold slate floor, a small square window with no glass, just a thick mesh to keep out flies. It makes me think of Nonna's house in the hills, only here the air is chilled and the wash of light from outside is greeny grey, not the warm yellow and gold of Nonna's place.

Stairs from the hall wind up to the bedrooms— four of them, dusty and faded with old-fashioned wooden bedsteads. I sit on one, and a cloud of dust rises from the old mattress. Under the bed I find zipped bags containing sheets and blankets. A mouse or something has chewed the corner of one. Everywhere there are old dried-up mouse droppings. The curtains at the windows are thick with dust and old cobwebs; the spiders died long ago.

This is a house that's been asleep for years, a fairy tale house that needs to be woken and shaken up and cleaned and made new and brought back to life. It seems impossible. Overwhelming. How can we possibly live here?

I go into the small bedroom at the side of the house, with a view over a sloping, green field with a single tree and a stone barn. I push the bottom sash window: it sticks at first and bits of loose putty flake off but then the wooden frame begins to slide up, and cold, clean air and the sound of birds and water rush into the chilly room.

The rain has stopped; everything is shining in early morning sunlight.

I can't bear to be inside the dusty, dark house any longer.

I shove my feet into a pair of ancient green boots by the back door that might once have belonged to my English grandmother, Frieda, who I never met. They're almost the right size.

I step outside, blink in the bright light. I take deep breaths of the clear, cold air. No human voices, or traffic sounds, nothing but birdsong and the rushing sound that must be the river Dad talked about. *The river has a voice*, he said. *You have to learn to listen to it*.

I splash through puddles to the gate. The other houses are all silent, empty. It's a ghost village. I don't belong here. The windows are like eyes, watching.

I walk away from the houses across the small, grassy square, follow the sound of the water and find a stone path sloping downhill towards the river. On my right there's the field with the tree and the barn that I saw from the bedroom window. A flock of bright birds lands in the tree, then lifts off again in one swirling, chattering swoop, a wave of birds. The light catches their feathery bellies, each a flash of white. They fly past the empty barn and disappear into a copse of trees beyond the river. I go after them, feet slipping on the wet stones. The cold air makes my eyes water. I feel safer, hidden among the trees.

I run down a series of stone steps onto a narrow wooden bridge. I stop to drop a bit of branch over the edge and watch it swirl and eddy in the rushing water, under the bridge and out the other side. I carry on up the path towards the wood where the birds went, my ears full of the sound of water. A stream tumbles down the hillside over a series of huge, flat rocks before dropping into the river below. A tiny bird dips and flits from one wet rock to another. It takes no notice of me. On I run, up the muddy path along the edge of the hill. I'm out of breath already; the path is steep, close to a rocky edge. I hold onto a branch of a small, crooked tree and peer over: it's a sheer drop, right down to the river. I close my eyes for a second and imagine it—the dizzy fall, the shock of flesh and bone on stone, the wash of the water carrying me downstream. I pull myself back to the path and walk on more carefully. All around is the rushing sound of water and wind.

Should I go further? Do I dare?

At Nonna's, the countryside was full of people— old people tending vines on the terraced hillsides, watering tomatoes in their gardens, cutting meadow hay with old-fashioned scythes, rounding up chickens, and tending goats. Everyone knew me because everyone knew Nonna.

Nothing like this cold, wet, empty place.

Be brave, I tell myself. *Walk on*.

The path dips into the dark shadow of pine trees planted close together, then widens out onto a smooth, grassy plateau, with higher hills and moorland beyond, going up, up, up. I keep going. At the end of the path there's a ruined farmhouse.

I pick my way over the damp stones leading to a door at the side. There's no actual door, just a wooden lintel above where one would have been, and a granite step. The wooden floor's rotten in places. Something skitters away in a dark corner: a mouse or a bat or something bigger?

I wait. Listen.

Birds' feet clatter on the slate roof. A huge black raven takes off with slow wing beats.

Light flows into the house through the broken windows, through gaps in the walls, and the spaces where the roof slates have slipped. I go round to the front of the house and sit on a stone that might have been part of a garden wall once upon a time.

Marta would love it here.

Whenever I think of her, my whole body aches.

The house is keeping watch over the land: I can see for miles, up to the hills all around, all the way down the gorge where the river has carved its way over thousands of years. Behind the house, there are piles of stones and a place where long ago someone has cut a way into the rock. An old mine shaft.

The ruined house sighs and creaks and rustles as if it's waiting for me to leave.

The wind drops. Mist creeps over the hill and blots out the sky. It beads my hair and skin and clothes. I shiver.

'I'm going now,' I say out loud. 'You win!'

A little way down the track, I hear a call—not a bird, more like a snatch of laughter. I wheel round, glimpse something pale flapping at the side of the house. Was there someone hiding there, after all?

The path is slippery. I keep back from the scary edge. Under the dark trees, the rushing river sounds loud and dangerous. There's no sign of the little bird when I get to the waterfall rocks. I clatter over the wooden bridge and up the path the other side to the house.

Our house that's not ours. Not mine, anyway. Not home.

Eight

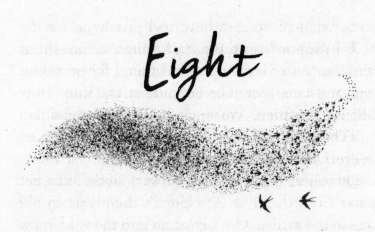

Dad's lying on the sofa exactly where I left him, still asleep. He doesn't even wake up when I stand right next to him. I stare at his face. He looks closed off. Unreachable.

But I'm hungry. We need a fire, and breakfast, and hot tea. Dad loves his tea.

I find wood and coal in the shed at the back of the house to make a fire in the kitchen stove. There are matches in a cardboard box in the drawer next to the cutlery. Nonna taught Gabriella and me how to lay a fire, starting with small bits of kindling, adding the bigger bits of wood and then coal once the flames are dancing. I should check the chimney for birds' nests, but I've no idea how, so I just hope for the best. I rummage in the bag of things we bought at the shop yesterday and fish out things for breakfast: eggs, and some sort of bread, and tea, and milk. How will we get more? We've no car, and it's miles and miles to that shop.

I turn the tap but nothing comes out.

Of course not. Nothing works. Maybe I can get water from the river. At Nonna's there was an old well in the garden. Out I go again into the wilderness at the back of the house to see if there's one here.

I search for a long time. The garden hasn't been tended for years. Winter snow and rain has flattened the grass and weeds and thistles. There's a patch of ground where vegetables might once have been grown, with a wall around, and at one edge ferns grow, a dash of bright green against the grey stone wall. When I get closer I find two wide, flat stone slabs, and smaller pebbles where a freshwater spring bubbles up out of the ground. Someone long ago has tied a metal cup to a hook in the wall with a rusty chain. I go back to the kitchen for a jug and use the cup to fill it with spring water. I heat it in a pan on the stove. Finally, I make tea and boil two eggs. I take everything on a tray to Dad.

'My lovely lass,' he whispers. He reaches his hand out toward me.

'Lass?' I say.

'The old word. What my parents would have called you.'

'You slept for a long time,' I say. 'I've been up for hours.'

He notices the tray for the first time. 'Thank you, love.'

He peels the shell off an egg and eats it, and slowly sips the tea. I eat my egg. He lies back again, as if eating has exhausted him. What's *wrong* with him? Is he getting sick?

'I've been outside,' I tell him. 'There's a spring, for water, in the garden . . . We should clean up the house next. It's all a mess. You can tell me about Grandma Frieda and what it was like when you lived here.'

He's not listening. His eyes have that glazed look again. He goes across to the door and up the stairs.

Practical things. Focus. That's what Mamma would say. *One step at a time.*

I have to do everything the old-fashioned way,

like Nonna used to. Sweep floors with a broom. Mop and bucket of water for the kitchen and bathroom floors. Everything takes ages. I have to go down to the spring each time to refill the bucket, scooping up the water with the little cup.

I sing as I go through the house. I sing the songs Marta and I like, and then Mamma's favourites. I go *lalala* when I don't remember the words. It's good to fill the house with sound. The only room I don't go into is the bedroom at the front. Dad's shut the door. I make loads of noise on the landing, to wake him up. Mamma would be furious if she knew he was sleeping all day while I did *everything*.

After a while, I can't stop my thoughts racing to all the impossible things. My phone battery's dead. There's no electricity here, so how will I get my phone to work ever again? Marta has no idea where I am. And that starts more worry bugs scrabbling in my head. Did she get home OK? Has she gone somewhere safe with her family, too? How will Mamma and Gabriella get here if there are no more trains?

I keep the words from that last text alive in my mind. They'll find a way to us somehow. 'I love you,

Mamma!' I speak the words out loud so the house can hear. I imagine the words floating out of the open windows and all the way back to her.

I open all the windows and let the cold air rush through the house. I beat the dust from the curtains. I drag the rugs outside into the yard and drape them over the gate to air. The mist has almost gone, just lingering along the river valley.

Dad's door stays shut.

I unpack the rest of the food and store it on the larder shelves. Tins. They'll keep. We should eat the fresh stuff first, the cheese and eggs and vegetables. I check in the stone jars lined along one of the shelves, but they're all empty. Dad's hopeless! Why didn't he buy flour for making bread? Pasta. Rice. Stuff that would last.

I go outside again to explore the sheds. There's an ancient loo in one, with ancient cobwebs and long-dead spiders and woodlice in the corners. The bigger shed has garden stuff. A stack of ancient newspapers, dry and yellowed with age. Old cloths. A wood store, half full. Garden tools hang on hooks along one side: fork, spade, rake, hoe, a curved scythe with a long wooden handle for cutting hay. It's so quiet.

The shed smells old, dusty, faintly sweet. Dust spins in the shafts of light through the open door. It's all so strange, standing here as if I've stepped into a different world completely. Swapped into some past life that belonged to people I never knew.

I go back into the kitchen.

Dad pads slowly down stairs. 'Oh! Isabella!' He stares at me. He'd forgotten I was here.

'I've been out in the garden,' I say. 'Are you OK?'

He nods. 'Much better, now.'

Good. Now he can be more like a dad again.

'Will you tell me about my Grandma Frieda?' I say.

'Tea, first,' Dad says. He goes to turn on the tap.

'No water,' I say.

I show him the spring in the garden. I fill the kettle using the little cup tied to the string. I put it on the stove to heat.

'If there's no running water, how will we flush the loo?'

'We'll have to use the old earth toilet with the soakaway,' Dad says. 'Like when these houses were first built. No sewers or running water in those days, either. But maybe we just need to turn it back on. Maybe it got turned off to stop the pipes freezing when Frieda and Tom left. The old man said something about the water.'

He rummages in a cupboard in the hall. Turns something, gets me to check the taps. But there's still no running water.

We make the tea. We carry it into the living room. Dad starts to talk about the past. His own childhood. The freedom: fishing, and messing about outside. Dens and tree houses. Swimming in the river. 'Almost feral,' he says. 'That's how it was with all of us. Everything changed when we were sent away to school. *Shades of the prison house . . .*' He smiles sadly. 'After that, I was free again, travelling across Europe. Discovered Italy: Rome, Verona, Sicily, Catania . . . Began drawing again. Met your beautiful mother . . .'

He's lost, day-dreaming the past.

I write my first letter to Marta.

Dear Marta,

I cannot believe it is only 4 days since I saw you. I keep thinking of that last time, when you turned and waved goodbye. And then I heard the explosions. The bomb at the tram station. Are you OK? I tried and tried to call you but your phone wasn't working. And then Mamma said I had to leave with Dad on the last train and so I couldn't tell you and didn't say goodbye or anything and I'm really sad about that. I think about you all the time. Are you safe? What are you doing?

The house here is old and damp. If you think of our sunny flat in town, and then imagine the total opposite, that is what it's like. Big and old and cold and dark. We have no electricity or phone or even running water. I have not had a shower for 4 days! If you were here with me it would be so much more fun, a bit like that time we went camping near the beach with your mum. Except there were showers there, and other people. There is literally NO ONE but Dad and me in the village and maybe the whole valley, and he is being even more weird than usual. OK, I know you like my Dad, and I love him really, but he's just vacant and tired all the time and doesn't do anything and it's SO FRUSTRATING (Ha! Maybe because he lived here when he was a boy he is reverting to childhood. I'm having to be the grown-up! That is actually what it's like.)

The world's gone crazy. We saw some horrible things on the journey but I'm not going to make you angry and sad by writing them here.

I've been exploring, when the rain stops (not often). There

are trees and fields and dry-stone walls and barns and birds
and a river and that's about it. I found a ruined farmhouse on
a hill. I will draw a picture of it for you on a sunny day. It is
unbelievably quiet all the time. Tell me about all the things you
are doing and how school is (If school is still happening????)
and also any news because we haven't a clue what is going on.
Nothing works here. I think Dad's shocked by how bad it is.

I will write to you everyday Marta. I miss you so much. I
hope you and your mum and nonna are safe. xxxxxxx

I study the photo of Marta and me. Dad took it on
his phone last year and printed it out, a copy for
each of us. It's faded and scruffy from being pinned
up in my bedroom. Our hair was shorter then. We're
wearing identical T-shirts. Arms around each other.
We could be twins. I peer more closely. We're on
our balcony, sunlight so bright it shows up the red
streaks in Marta's dark hair.

Miss you, I whisper to her.

Nine

I've been sitting for ages on the window seat in the dining room. Dad's drawing me: quick sketches in pencil on thick white paper. I wriggle and squirm, longing to stretch and run free.

'Please don't fidget,' Dad says. He leans forward, tucks a strand of dark hair behind my ear. 'Nearly done.'

Every day so far it has rained. Every day, I have written a letter to Marta. My plan is that I will post them all to her one day soon. I just have to work out how. I have told her about the house, and about the river, and the strange quietness of this place. And how much I miss her.

Today is the first time since we arrived that Dad's done any drawing. I guess there's no point. How will he get any work here?

'Can I see?' I ask.

'Later, maybe.'

He's drawing bits of me—an ear, my nose, my hand resting on the seat.

'What's it for?'

'It's not *for* anything,' Dad says. 'Just drawing.'

A flock of birds takes off from the big tree in the field.

Dad holds the pencil mid-air. He's watching too. 'Fieldfares.' He smiles at me. 'Remember the starlings? You loved them when you were little.'

Of course I remember! As soon as he says the word they fly into my mind. I've always had a thing about birds. Dad's the same.

Back when I was too young to walk home from school by myself, Dad would meet me at the end of the day, and in winter we would always stop on the big river bridge to watch the starlings. They soared and swooped and turned together in huge flocks, weaving patterns like scarves, like mist, like shoals of fish, dark against the sky as it paled from blue to turquoise and green and pink and gold as the sun went down. And we'd be amazed at all the people scurrying home from school and work, *not* looking skywards to watch the dance of the starlings. Because how could anyone resist something so beautiful and strange and wild in the sky above them, in the middle of the city?

'How come they never bump into each other? How come they all swerve at the same time? Why do they do it at all?' I'd ask, but Dad never had any answers.

Dad snaps the sketchbook shut. He puts the pencils neatly back in the tin. 'Enough for today. Thank you, Isabella.'

I jump down from the window seat.

Dad walks slowly into the hall and up the creaking stairs, that familiar distracted look on his face. The bedroom door clicks shut. He's probably forgotten all about me already. But at least he's drawing again. That's a start. It's what Mamma always tells him. *Go and draw, Daniel. You'll feel like yourself again.* Maybe Dad will be more like a proper dad soon.

The ruined house high on the hill is like a magnet, pulling me in. This will be my third visit. Yesterday it was raining too hard to stay for long. I was scared I might slip over the path edge on the way down. Dad doesn't have a clue where I go. No one would know what had happened to me.

Today there's no rain, but the river is swollen, brown with earth and stones washed down off the hills. Bits of tree and boulders bump and swirl in the rushing water. I go over the bridge and up the slippery path.

Sun breaks through the cloud. Everything gleams in the sudden light. The trees are alive with the flutter and chatter of small birds. I climb higher.

The raven takes off from the roof of the ruined house as soon as I get there.

Inside, the wooden floors are all out of kilter, like the rolling deck of a ship at sea. The angles of the windows and doors are all wrong. The house is quietly slipping into the earth. But it's dry inside, and almost warm. I settle down on the floor in the middle of the room and listen to the deep silence.

Sunlight slants through the gaps in the walls, reaches into the farthest corners. Nothing dark or scary. An old tin bath hangs on a nail on one wall, but that's the only sign of the people who once lived here.

There's a flash of colour outside; movement.

A fox! It trots across the garden in front of the house, intent on its own business. It sniffs the stones, digs at a corner of the old garden. It sits for a while and scratches, like a dog. It takes no notice of me, doesn't seem to hear or smell my presence in the house, or maybe it knows I'm no danger. It curls up in the sun and sleeps.

The fox lifts its head, sniffs the air. It springs up, ears pricked to listen, and lopes off down towards the river and the cover of trees.

I listen too.

There are voices! Someone's coming!

I scrabble up and peer through the broken window at the back of the house.

Two figures are walking along a narrow track along the ridge of the hill; a boy, maybe a bit older than me, and a younger girl in a pale skirt. It flaps as she balances over a wooden bridge at the top of a stream. The boy holds something in one hand. He calls out to the girl.

I shrink back from the window. They're coming this way, the girl running ahead.

My heart beats faster. So, there are other people here, after all!

'She's in the house, silly!' The boy's voice rings out, soft and strange like the old man in the van, but easier to understand.

The small girl picks her way over the stones in the garden.

I wait in the doorway.

She stops when she sees me. 'There you are! Hello!'

'Hello,' I say, suddenly awkward.

The boy appears. He hangs back. The thing he's holding is a freshly-dead rabbit.

The girl keeps talking, a stream of words. 'We saw you come up the path but you didn't see us! And we saw you another day and then we didn't see you because it was raining and you never came up. You're the first new person.' She hardly stops for breath.

'I didn't see you,' I say.

'Did you meet the fox just now?' she asks.

I nod.

'That's my fox,' she says. 'What's your name?'

'Isabella. What's yours?'

'Kelda. It means spring or well.'

'That's nice.'

'You talk funny!'

'So do you!'

She laughs. 'No I don't! Why do you sound like that?'

The boy steps closer. He's watching me like a hawk.

'Like what? Not like you, I suppose. Because I don't come from around here.'

'Where do you come from then? Are you on your own like us? Or are there more? We've only seen one of you. You mustn't tell anyone about us ever ever ever. You have to promise. We brought you food today in case you were hungry.'

The boy holds out the rabbit.

It looks disgusting, but I know I should say thank you. It's meat, after all. It's the same as eating meat from a shop except you have to think about it being a real animal that had its own life and now is dead.

'Thank you,' I say. 'But we've got food. We brought tins and stuff with us.'

The girl looks at her brother. I *guess* he's her brother.

'We?' he says.

'Me and my dad.'

He looks around nervously.

'Dad's not here now,' I say. 'He's back in the house. In the village.'

'Oh,' he says slowly. 'Well, this is a good rabbit, lots of meat.'

I nod. 'Thank you. I . . . what do I do with it? I mean, I've never skinned a rabbit . . .' The idea of cutting into fur and skin and bone makes me feel sick.

'I'll show you,' he says. 'You need to learn, if you are living here. We have chickens too and can trade eggs.'

Trade for what? I don't have anything to give him in return.

'We'll not be staying here long,' I say. Even as the words come out of my mouth I know it's not true. I've no idea how long we will be here.

The girl's playing some sort of game, hopping from one stone to another, singing to herself. She looks like someone from olden times with her funny flappy skirt, woolly jumper, laced leather boots and her hair in pigtails.

'Do you live near?' I ask the boy.

He pauses, as if he's deciding something.

'You must tell no one. Not your dad, even, not anyone. Promise?'

I nod. 'OK.'

'Top of Swinner Gill.' He nods his head as if to show me the direction. 'Over Swallow Fell.'

'And are there many other people in your village?'

He laughs. ''T'isn't a village, 'tis an old field barn we made into home.'

'All alone all alone with the foxes and the buzzards!' the little girl sings.

'You mustn't tell. We'll be taken away if people find out.'

I nod, even though I don't understand. 'So, where's everyone gone? Why are the houses all empty?'

The boy stares at me again. 'You don't know?'

I shake my head. I feel stupid.

'Everyone left the valley after the sickness came. Our mam and da died from it.'

I stare at him. 'Sorry.' I swallow hard. 'What kind of sickness?'

'The sickness that came three year ago. It spread up the valley. Almost everyone died. No one was allowed to stay. They rounded up the remaining children.' He pauses. 'Said the water was poisoned.'

'The water?' I say.

'The water in the taps and pipes. It got turned off.'

'We've been drinking from the spring in the garden,' I say. 'Will we get sick?'

'Spring water bubbles up fresh from deep down. You'll be fine.'

I nod.

Why doesn't Dad know any of this?

'I've got to go now,' I say. 'You should keep your rabbit. We've got eggs and cheese and stuff at our house.'

'And you won't tell your dad you saw us?'

'No.'

'Promise?'

'Promise.'

'Goodbye, Isabella! Come back tomorrow!' The little girl waves.

She calls out after me in her sing-song voice. 'His name is Rowan, seeing as he didn't tell you and you didn't ask!'

Ten

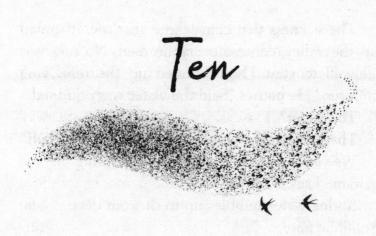

Kelda and Rowan. Kelda meaning well or spring, and Rowan like the tree. I can't stop thinking about them, but I don't say anything to Dad. I promised I wouldn't. But I write it all down in today's letter to Marta. I didn't promise I wouldn't write it in a letter.

I study the large map framed on the wall in the dining room. I find this village easily enough and then I trace a finger along the blue line of the river and up the other side. I find the names *Swallow Fell* and *Swinner Gill Lead Mine*. The dotted green line of a footpath goes behind the ruined house and along a ridge of hill. The brown lines are contours to show you how steep the hillside is: the closer together they are, the steeper the edge. So, steep.

Dad comes and stands beside me. 'Beautiful, isn't it? Your grandfather framed that old map.' He sighs. 'Even when I was a child, people were moving away. Too hard a life. No work. Now everyone's gone. Not a single person left.'

How can I tell Dad the real reason, without mentioning Rowan and Kelda?

'What if something's happened here? Something bad,' I say.

'An accident, you mean? The old man mentioned something.'

'Yes. And that's why the water had to be turned off. And no one could live here. Maybe it isn't safe.'

'I'd have heard,' Dad says.

'How? You haven't been here for years. Who would have told you?'

Dad goes quiet.

'When did you last visit?'

'Nine years ago. Your grandmother's funeral.' He shakes his head. 'I can't believe it was that long ago.'

'She died here?'

'Not in the house. She'd been in hospital for a while.'

'What was she like?'

Dad thinks for a moment. 'Kind. She loved the wildness. She'd have loved you, Isabella. Gabriella too, of course. But especially you.'

'Did you tell her about us?'

'Of course. Showed her photos. But she was old, losing her memory by then.'

'And she never came to visit us.'

'No. She was too frail. Hardly left the house. Hardly travelled anywhere her whole life. Couldn't understand why I chose to live in another country so far away.' Dad sighs again. 'I should have brought you here before. It's part of who you are. Another thing I've messed up.'

'Stop it, Dad! We're here now, aren't we?'

'But it's not the place I grew up. The country I knew. Nearly ten years of division and decline and neglect and this is what you get.' He takes a deep breath. 'At least there are no bombs. No actual war. We're still safer here.'

Dad trails back upstairs.

He doesn't ask what I'm going to do for the rest of the day.

Part of who you are.

I've never really thought about it like that. I know it's why Dad's always spoken with us in English, to keep that connection. But it's never felt like who I *am*. Not really.

I escape outside.

Kelda's playing some sort of game in and out of the ruined house. I'm out of puff by the time I get there. I sit down on one of the stones in the garden. She doesn't say anything at first: she carries on singing, balancing on the tumbledown garden wall and jumping off at the gap where a gate would have been. She winces.

'You could break an ankle doing that!'

She laughs. 'You sound like my brother.'

'Is he here?'

'No.'

She sits down near me. She's so little to be here all by herself. What must her life be like? No parents, no one but her brother. Living off rabbits and eggs, making a home in a barn.

'If we sit very quietly my fox might come and visit.'

'OK.'

'But it might not if it sees you. It doesn't know you yet.'

'I could hide inside the house, if you want. I did that before, when the fox came.'

She shakes her head. 'Stay here.'

She shifts closer to me. We wait. Nothing happens.

The wind makes a rushing sound in the trees, like the rush of river water. Tiny streams trickle down the hillside, join together to make a bigger stream that tumbles and falls down the hill to the river in the valley bottom.

High in the sky, a hawk hovers.

Kelda comes closer still. She puts her small hand on my arm. The skin is grubby and lined and rough, the hand of someone much older. The nails are bitten short.

She looks at me with her solemn eyes. 'Is your mam dead too?'

Her question shocks me. Out of the blue like that!

'NO! She's fine, she'll come here as soon as she can bring my big sister and we'll be together like a proper family again.' I blink back tears.

Kelda strokes my arm very gently.

'Who is your sister?' she asks. 'What's she called?'

'Gabriella. She's nineteen, grown up. She's my *half*-sister, really. My mum had her before she met my dad. She's away at university.'

Kelda says the word slowly aloud. She's never heard it before.

'Like school. Where you go away to study when you're older. She's doing History . . .' I stop there. It's too complicated to explain.

Kelda wanders off.

'Come and see where we live,' she calls. 'We've got new kittens.'

'I found these places on a map,' I tell her as I follow behind on the narrow path along the ridge.

She doesn't answer. She doesn't know what a map is. Why would she?

'Don't look down or you get giddy,' she says.

But of course I do.

We're above the treeline. Above the ruined house. Above the old lead mine and the heaps of spoil. My head reels at so much space and air below as well as above. I could drop a pebble and watch it tumble down all the way to the river.

I steady myself, and follow the flap of Kelda's skirt as she skips way ahead.

Instead of grass either side of the path there's dried heather and moss and bog. And soon we're winding downhill towards an old stone barn in the middle of a field.

The boy, Rowan, watches us from lower down the field.

It's dark inside. It smells of smoke and something cooking. My eyes adjust. The barn's divided into two, and one side there's dried grass piled on a kind of wooden platform, and this side, just bare earth on the floor, and two wooden chairs, a table, and some sort of home-made stove with a chimney to take the smoke up through a gap in the roof. A pot on the stove. A bucket of water. It's very neat and tidy but there's hardly anything here.

'We brought the chairs and table from our old house,' Kelda says proudly. 'And cups and plates and bowls and a bucket and the pots for the stove. And a broom to sweep the floor. That's my job. And tools for making and growing things.'

'Where do you sleep?'

'In the hayloft. It's really warm, just a bit scratchy. We cut new hay in the summer. We couldn't bring blankets in case they carried the sickness. Rowan stitched us a rabbit-fur cover.'

A raggedy brown hen scratches at the earth near the door. It comes right inside. The boy shoos it out again.

'Come and see the kittens. They're only just born,' Kelda says.

I follow her into the other half of the barn. We have to go outside again and round to another entrance. On the floor in one corner, a tabby and white cat rests on a pile of old sacks. She lifts her head and watches us, but stays lying down.

Kelda sits with me, cross-legged on the earth floor. The barn smells sweet and dusty, the scent of dried grass.

Three tiny kittens creep out from under the mother cat's furry chest. One tabby, two black and white. The mother cat purrs loudly as they paddle with tiny paws against her belly and start feeding. They're small as mice. Eyes tight shut.

'Oh! They're perfect!'

Kelda smiles. 'Yes. We saw them being born. Maybe you can have one when they're big enough. Rowan says we can't keep so many cats. They're half wild. Some cats got left behind when the people left the village. They find mice and rats and voles to eat. Birds, too. But this one, the mother cat, she's ours. We brought her with us when we came here. She's called Flora.'

A shadow. The boy's standing in the doorway.

'They'll not be ready to leave their mother for months,' he says. 'Isabella won't be here by then, Kelda.'

'Won't you?' She looks at me, disappointed.

'Probably not,' I say quickly. 'Though, when Mum and my sister come we might decide to stay here longer. I don't know. Dad says we're safer here.'

'Safer from what?'

'The bombs. The war.'

He nods.

The three of us watch the kittens. The mother cat licks them tail to nose. They squirm and make tiny mewling sounds and all the time, she purrs as if she loves them and they make her happy. The last time I saw newborn kittens was at Nonna's. She loved cats, but Mamma wouldn't let us have one, however much I pleaded. *Not in a city flat*, she said. *That's not fair on the cat. Even a pet cat deserves a wild life outdoors.*

'I made meat stew,' Rowan says. 'Do you want some with us, Isabella?'

'Yes please,' I say. 'If there's enough.'

I follow him outside.

My name sounds strange, the way he says it. Not like my name at all. The meat stew tastes good. It's hot and so much better than the old cheese and bread and tinned beans we've been eating. Rowan makes sure Kelda washes her hands, and sits down at the table. He makes her eat every scrap in her bowl. There is something so tender and touching about the way he takes care of her. Mostly, it's Kelda who talks, and Rowan who listens. I ask her how old she is and she says she isn't sure but Rowan says she's nearly seven.

'How long have you been living here like this?'

She looks to her brother. 'Two years or three?'

He nods. 'Nearly three.'

'It's too long ago. I don't remember it,' she says. 'I was little. I can't remember our mam and da's faces really but we have a picture, don't we Rowan, and sometimes we talk to them in the picture. And Rowan tells me the story, about how they got sick. Lots of people got sick at the same time and almost everyone else left but our family, and then our mam died and Da said we had to hide in the barn and he helped us get things we might need and he said people would make us leave the valley and any children who survived would have to live in a house for Special Children. So we hid. And people came and took Da away too after that but we were all right. They didn't know we were hiding in the barn.' She doesn't sound sad, just factual.

'I don't understand,' I say. 'What do you mean, *Special Children?*'

Rowan sighs. 'We're children who survived the sickness, aren't we? So that means we've got some kind of immunity.' He puts his hands over Kelda's ears so she can't hear what he says next. 'They'd want to find out why. My father was afraid they'd use us for *experiments*. So we have to stay hidden.'

Kelda struggles free. 'Don't DO that!'

'Enough talking,' Rowan says. 'Isabella doesn't need to hear any more about us.'

There's silence while we finish eating. Kelda licks her bowl clean.

Rowan takes the dishes outside. The hens make a gentle crooning sound as he goes past.

'I'm really sorry about your mum and dad,' I tell Kelda. 'But I'm glad you and Rowan didn't get sick.'

'We're just lucky. Lucky lucky lucky!' She climbs off the chair and goes outside, singing the words over and over.

I follow her outside.

Rowan's washing the dishes in a bucket.

'You've got a well!'

He nods. 'All the field barns had wells, so they could draw water for the cows over winter. Each barn housed four or five cows in the old days.'

'I should go now,' I say. 'I thought . . . maybe if you have spare eggs, I could bring blankets tomorrow, as a swap.'

Kelda smiles. 'That's good, isn't it, Ro? Yes?'

'The blankets were sealed up in bags,' I say. 'They won't make you sick. It was a long time ago that my grandparents left the house. The house has been shut up for years.'

'OK. Tomorrow. Six eggs, one blanket. That's fair.'

Eleven

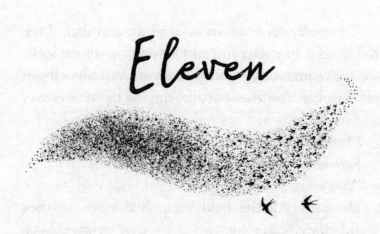

Dear Marta,

Maybe I have stepped into Grandma Frieda's boots after all, like that story we read at school ("walk one hundred miles in someone else's shoes", remember?). Our old life already seems so far away. I'm getting used to the new things I have to do here, like fetching water and eking out the food store and secretly trading things with Rowan and Kelda. We have heard nothing about Mamma and Gabriella. (Or you.)

I think about you all the time.

There's so much space in this house. Spare bedrooms. You could talk to your mum about coming here too. It would be so much better with you here.

Each day there are signs of things changing. The river level has gone down. There are yellow catkins on the trees along the bank. The birds seem to sing louder in the early morning, as soon as it gets light. The days are longer. Dad gets up late, he drifts about the house, he spends most of the time upstairs with the door shut. And then this morning he came into the kitchen and said we should do something about the garden. 'Plant seeds,' he said. 'Grow some vegetables so we don't die of scurvy.'

Apparently scurvy is what you get when you don't eat enough vitamin C. Sailors on long voyages used to get it, before people discovered about lemons and limes. We can't grow lemons or limes here, it's too cold and wet, but we can grow vegetables like beans and salad and carrots.

I AM SO HAPPY that Dad is at last deciding things and DOING something! He's going to walk to that shop I told you about to get seeds and food. It's about 25 miles each way so he has to stay overnight. He is also going to try phoning Mamma from there to find out what is going on and when she will arrive here. I didn't want to go with him. I said I would stay here by myself and we had a horrible fight about that, but I won. (He doesn't know about Rowan and Kelda. I can't tell him that I'll be with them in the daytime.) It's only for one night.

I will actually be scared but I didn't tell him that because I so wanted him to go. We desperately need more food. I made a list so he gets the right things this time. Stuff that will last, like dried beans and lentils and porridge oats and pasta (Ha! Bet you wish you could eat beans and lentils and porridge! Not!).

He's been driving me mad. It's about time he took some initiative and acted like a DAD! I see why Mamma gets so frustrated with him.

Anyway. He finally left. He walked up the track. He turned and waved when he got to the proper road and suddenly that made me really sad. I ran up the track after him, and hugged him and he held me close and it was really hard to let him go.

I watched him getting smaller and smaller in the distance till he was just a dot, and then I could no longer see him at all.

The house seems really empty without him.

When I'm writing to you, Marta, it's like we're talking, and I'm not quite so lonely. xxxxxxx

I stand at the front window for a long time, unable to move. I stare at the empty road. I go over and over that moment when Dad was just a dot in the distance, and then nothing at all. Walking back into the empty house; how everything looked strange and different, because Dad was no longer here.

I wander from room to room. There's a weird hush over everything. The tiniest creak makes me jump.

I open the windows to let in the birdsong and the sound of the river.

I hesitate outside Dad's shut door and then I open it wide and step right in. I've not been in here since we first arrived.

It's full of shadow: the curtains are half closed. I yank them back and open the window.

The room's a mess. The bed covers are jumbled in a heap, paper is strewn all over the table, screwed-up pieces on the wooden floor underneath. His drawing pens and papers are scattered everywhere as if he swept them off with his arm and couldn't be bothered to tidy anything up.

I kneel down, pick them up, stack the papers neatly, line up the pens. I pick up the waste paper and put it in the bin.

On impulse I smooth out one of the scrunched-up balls. It's a drawing, a pencil sketch of a person who that looks a little like me, and a lot like Mum. I study it. What was he thinking? I scrunch it up again and throw it away.

Through the open window a bird calls from the garden. The same notes, over and over, calling me outside. I take a small tin of coloured pencils from Dad's desk. I fetch my sketchbook from the dining room table. I put on the old coat and shove the tin and the book deep in the pocket. It's a relief to leave the echoing, empty house behind.

The raven is perched on the roof of the ruined house. It doesn't fly off. I sit on a stone in the old garden and listen to the river far below, and a buzzard calling high above the hill. All over the grass there are new spring flowers, small bright yellow ones like stars, and small white violets with heart-shaped faces.

The sun feels warm. No Kelda playing here today. I wait and wait, and still there is no sign of her.

The fox visits, briefly. It runs along the ridge, starts to cross towards the ruined house then stops and sniffs the air. It changes track and lopes away again, a streak of red against the dry grass and heather of the fell. *Fell* is the word Rowan and Kelda use for these hills. And a waterfall is a *force*. *Gill* means a ravine or a small river, from the old Norse word *gil*. Rowan doesn't go to school but he knows so many things.

I walk along the footpath, cross over Swinner Gill on the rickety bridge and go carefully along the ridge of Swallow Fell. A flock of small brown birds take flight ahead of me with a sudden whirr of wings. A bird of prey floats on the thermal air currents high above. The higher I go, the lighter I feel.

Rowan and Kelda are working in the field near the barn. I wave as I come down the slope. Kelda puts her too-big spade down on the ground and runs over. She hugs me tight and it feels so lovely. I hold her close.

'Hello!' I say. 'You're busy! I thought you might be playing at the ruined house. I saw your fox.'

'Good! Did it come close? Is it getting used to you?'

'No. It ran away. So, what are you doing?'

'We're getting ready for planting. It's time, now, Rowan says. The earth's warming up.'

'What will you grow here?'

Rowan stops digging for a moment. 'Potatoes. Beans and peas. We saved the seed from last year's crop.'

'How do you know how to do all this?'

'How else would we live? You can eat wild dandelion and nettles and sorrel and watercress but they don't fill you up like potatoes and beans.'

'My dad's walking all the way to the town today,' I say. 'To get us food and seeds and things from the shop, and to phone my mother.'

Rowan looks up sharply.

'I haven't told him about you. Don't worry, it's OK.'

He glances down towards where the road must be. Would Dad be able to see this field from there? I don't think so.

'He's been gone a while,' I say. 'Even if he did see you, my dad wouldn't say anything. And he'd be pleased you were living here.'

'What is a shop?' Kelda kneels down on the earth and picks up a snail. She moves it into the longer grass. 'Your new home,' she whispers.

'Where you can buy things you need, like food and stuff. It's very far away,' I tell her.

'You never said there was a shop,' she says to Rowan.

He sighs. 'You know we have to stay hidden. Everyone would talk if they saw us in a shop. They'd ask questions. If adults find out about us, they won't let us stay here together. Anyway, we don't have any money. And we have everything we need without any shop. Don't talk about it again.'

'I'm tired of digging,' Kelda says. 'It's too hard.'

'Do something else, then. It's dinner time soon.'

'I brought something to show you,' I tell her. 'Can we go inside? We need the table.'

Rowan carries on digging.

Inside the barn, I show Kelda the pencils and paper. I draw her, and she watches intently, and laughs, and then she picks up a pencil and begins to make marks of her own. She tries out all the colours. She scribbles small circles and then bigger and bigger ones, till the page is covered and there is no white space left. She laughs when the colours flow over each other and make new colours. She is completely entranced.

I look around the barn. There are no pictures, no pens, no books. Just the one photo of her parents, grubby at the edges where they have held it so many times. This is the first time Kelda has held a pencil and done a drawing of her own.

When Rowan comes inside, she holds it up to show him.

He glances at me. He smiles at Kelda. 'Good,' he says. 'Better than digging, yes?'

He puts the big cooking pan onto the stove-top, lifts the lid and sniffs. He feeds more wood inside the belly of the stove. 'Pigeon stew. Lots of small bones, so be careful. It won't take long to heat up. Stay for dinner.'

'How do you catch a pigeon?' I ask, when we're all eating at the table. Rowan has to stand, to let me sit down. There are only two chairs.

'You trick them,' he says. 'They'll do anything for food. Rabbits, I snare. The trouble with a snare is you might catch the wrong thing. And you must check it every few hours, so you never leave an animal in pain. We pick berries and nuts. There are lots of wild plants you can eat. Mushrooms, too, in the autumn. And we have the hens and eggs.'

'You don't have milk or cheese or anything like that.'

'Not now. We kept a half-wild sheep for a while, but she got away. Once, there would have been sheep all over these fells. But it's not good for the land. They graze everything, including all the small tree seedlings; it's much better without them. More trees mean better soil, less erosion, cleaner air. Better for the land, better for people too. This is what should be happening all over the world, but it isn't. People don't like change.'

'Why not?'

'They find it hard to imagine doing things differently. Kelda and me, we didn't have a choice. Maybe that's the only way to make change happen.'

Mamma talks like this. She'd like Rowan. I wish I could tell her about him and Kelda.

Kelda's gone very quiet. She's practically falling asleep at the table. Rowan picks her up and carries her into the hayloft.

'She likes the soft blanket,' he says when he comes back.

'There's plenty of other stuff in our house,' I tell him. 'You could visit me, while Dad's away. Come and see what else you might need. Ours is the big house at the end of the village. You could stay all night and sleep on a proper bed and be comfortable.'

'We're fine as we are. We don't need things from your house. We don't need anything. We've managed all this time.'

'I'm sorry for saying about the shop,' I say. 'I didn't think.'

'No, you didn't.' He looks right at me. 'There won't be a phone. There's no electricity anywhere any more. There's no way to phone your mother.'

I blink back tears.

'A letter?' I say. 'Is there a way of sending a letter?'

He shrugs. 'Doubt it. Nothing's been working here for a long time.'

He goes outside and picks up the spade and starts digging. I take the dishes out to the well, fill the bucket, rinse them clean. I put everything back in the barn.

I'm sorry for making him upset. But he can't keep Kelda hidden and ignorant of the world forever. It isn't right.

I go out again to help him dig, but I'm not much good at it. Rowan has to go over my bit of ground and do it more thoroughly, deeper, getting all the roots out. I'm too hot, and the soil sticks to my boots and makes every step heavy.

I stop for a moment to stretch out my spine.

'Did you go to school, before?' I ask him.

'Before what?'

'Before the . . . the sickness.'

'Yes,' he says. 'Further down the valley. Only nine children. One teacher.'

'And Kelda?'

'No. She was too young.'

'Don't you miss all the people? Isn't it lonely, just you and Kelda?'

He doesn't answer. He carries on digging in a steady rhythm, as if it's easier than talking. The spade cuts a clean line into the turf; he turns it to reveal the dark earth beneath. He shakes the grass free, and picks out the white fleshy roots and lays them aside.

I put down the spade. 'Well, I'm going now. Thanks for the dinner. Say goodbye to Kelda for me.'

He nods. He carries on digging.

I climb back up the fell path.

Twelve

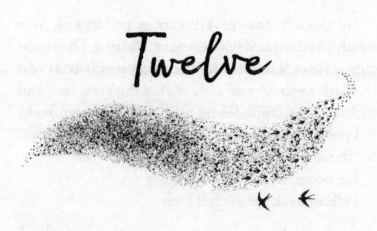

Dear Mamma,

I think about you every day. I hope you are safe. When are you coming here? We really miss you. It's so quiet. No one lives in any of the villages any more, there are no shops nearby, no electricity or buses or schools or phones or internet or radio or ANYTHING.

I cross that out. I begin again.

Can we come back home now? Have the explosions and bombs stopped? We are so cut off here, we have no idea what is happening in the rest of the world! Dad misses you. I miss you. We love you . . . I miss everyone. Have you heard anything from Marta? It's not good for Dad to be here without anyone to talk to. I am afraid he is getting ill again because he is lonely and missing you and not working . . . But today he's walking to the town to try to phone you and that's good.

Where are you?

Please write us a letter and send it to the shop and we can collect it from there . . . Tell us when you and Gabriella will get here and we will find a way to meet you at the station.

Nothing sounds right.

I long to tell her about Rowan and Kelda and the life they're living here, so frugal and careful and in step with nature. I push the paper and pens away from me and go into the kitchen. I check the stove is still alight. We have to be very careful not to let it go out completely because there are so few matches left. I have no idea what time it is. The day seems to pass very slowly.

I go out to the shed to find the garden tools. I take a fork and a spade and carry them over to the patch where once there was a vegetable garden. It's thick with grass and weeds. For Rowan and Kelda, their patch of garden means food, and survival. I start digging. It takes ages to clear just one tiny patch. My back aches, my legs ache. In the past, I would have given up, but things have to be different now.

What Rowan said about change . . . The life we were living, it couldn't carry on that way. It's all the things Mamma talks and writes about. The stuff people simply throw away, always wanting new things. The divide between the people who have everything, and those with almost nothing. The people fleeing war, and famine, and drought, and the governments and armies and guards who try to keep them out. The way money all over the world is spent on weapons, hurting instead of helping and healing. Her words are in my head, part of me. I understand it all better, now.

Gradually, I relax into the rhythm of digging. By the time it is beginning to get dark, I have cleared a whole patch that will be nearly ready for planting seeds when Dad gets back tomorrow.

For the hundredth time, I long to run a hot bath and soak in it for hours, listening to my music and chatting on my phone to Marta. Instead I have to fill the biggest pan with water from the spring and heat in on the stove and it's barely enough to wash in. I boil an egg for tea but there's no bread. It's lonely eating supper without Dad. Has he reached the town, yet? Where will he stay?

I go to bed as soon as it's dark, because there's nothing else to do. I light the candle in the lantern and put it on the bedside chest. I leave the curtains open so I can see the stars. Shadows dance around the room.

I blow out my candle and lie in the dark.

Never in my whole life have I been so completely alone.

Kelda and Rowan are more than a mile away, sleeping in the hayloft in their barn.

I wish I'd gone with Dad.

I can't sleep.

I go to the window seat, open the window wide and listen to the night. The river makes a roaring sound, endlessly flowing down the valley as it makes its journey from the high fells to the sea. The hunting owl floats across the field on silent wings. Another kind of night bird calls from the tree.

I climb back into bed. I try to imagine what Dad's doing—sleeping where? There are no hotels. Has someone offered him a bed for the night? *Is* there anyone? Is he huddled in some old barn, cold and alone?

My heart's racing. I'm still wide awake.

I retrace my old journey to and home from school: the shops and the people and the churches and the square with the fruit and flower market.

Bombs. The bitter smell. Sirens. *Marta . . .*

No, not that.

Happy things. My bedroom at home with its yellow walls and sunshine flooding through the open shutters. Dad, Mamma, Gabriella, Marta and me eating dinner on the balcony, and the swifts and swallows skimming the rooftops in the golden evening light.

The rise and fall of voices, people outside the cafés and bars in our street. The buzz of traffic further away. Crickets chirring in the flowering hibiscus trees on the corner of the square. Antonia practising scales on her flute. The church bell striking eight . . .

Already, that life seems so far away and so long ago.

I'm a different version of me.

I wake with the light and the birdsong. *Dad will be home today!*

I get dressed and go down to the kitchen, fill the kettle from the spring. A robin flies off from the patch I dug yesterday. The air's cool and fresh. Dad will be setting off from wherever he slept last night, walking back here. Maybe Rowan was wrong, and Dad did manage to phone Mamma, and he'll come back with a message from her. It's easier to feel hopeful in the daylight.

Kelda and Rowan will be up too, making whatever it is they have for breakfast. I'm hungry, but all we've got is tinned fruit and dry biscuits. So that's what I eat. It's hard to settle to anything. Even though I know Dad won't be here for hours I keep checking the road. I fetch logs from the pile in the shed and put them near the stove to dry. The wood store is getting smaller. I need to learn how to use an axe. How to saw wood. The best way to stack it to dry. The things we learned in school hardly seem relevant any more. Is school even happening, back home?

Marta. Marta. Marta. I miss you!

I take the sketchbook and pencils with me down the path to the river bridge and settle myself on one of the flat rocks at the edge of the waterfall. It smells of damp and moss and river water, of leaves and wet grass and wet rock. I sit so quietly the birds forget I'm here.

The small bird I saw the first time flits onto one of the boulders in the waterfall. It bobs and dips into the water, flies to a different stone, bobs and dips again. It walks right into the water, under the water, appears again, preens and warbles a song from another stone. I sketch its round shape and small tail, colour the chestnut brown feathers and white bib. It flies off to the river below, a whirr of wings, calls *stik-stik* as it flits.

Drawing makes me pay attention to things. I see more. It's one thing I can do here. With practice I'll get better at it. Marta will be pleased. She always tells me I'm good at drawing and writing, even though I'm not really. But that's just how Marta is: encouraging and kind and lovely.

I don't want to go far from the house today. I need to be here when Dad gets back. I go back and clear more weeds from the vegetable patch. My legs still ache from yesterday's digging so I don't keep at it for long. Inside the house, I wander the empty rooms. I feed more wood into the stove to keep it going. There are no more matches: I used the last ones to light the candles last night. Stupid.

I pull down books from the shelf in the sitting room, search for something interesting to read. I flip through an old book about this valley, with black and white photos and drawings. I find a photo of my water bird: it's called a dipper. I write the name under my drawing.

Still Dad doesn't come. I can't bear to sit here waiting any longer.

I put the thick coat on, and the boots, and walk up the track to the main road to meet Dad on his way back.

To begin with, it's fun retracing the way we came in the van. In daylight it all looks different.

The fields above the road all have ancient stone barns, like Rowan and Kelda's. Water tumbles from the fells down to the river. I get to the place where a stream crosses the road and wade through.

I go past three empty farmhouses. Another mile or so and I come to a small village with a whole row of stone houses with blank windows like dead eyes. The gardens are overgrown and wild. What if there are still dead people in some of the houses? Or I can catch the disease they died from? Is three years long enough ago? Ancient tractors and farm machinery rust in the abandoned farmyards. Everything smells of damp and decay.

Ahead, the road dips and climbs again but it's mostly straight, now—and there's still no sign of Dad.

Something catches my eye—a flash of light or movement, high on the fell above the abandoned village. I strain my eyes but it's too far off to see. What if there was someone living up there? But it was probably a bird. Or a wild sheep. Or sunlight reflected off water. This is a place of water—springs and streams and waterfalls and the river carving through the limestone for millions of years.

I sit on a dry-stone wall to rest and catch my breath.

What if Dad's hurt himself? Fallen and broken his ankle . . . he can't walk . . . he's got to wait for someone to find him and give him a lift, but there won't be anyone. No one comes here any more . . .

Or the shop's shut. Or he's heard something terrible from Mamma and has to travel on somewhere else. There are no buses or cars or taxis and he has to walk miles more, with no food and not much money . . .

My brain whirls and spirals and doubles back, a maze of horrible thoughts.

Stop it!

It will be getting dark soon.

There's no point going any further.

I give up.

I trudge back along the road the way I came, though the abandoned village, past the empty houses and farms. I look out for Kelda and Rowan's barn when I get closer, but the folds of the hills mean I can't see it from here. I walk on down the track to our house.

Loneliness wraps tighter around me, a heavy dark cloak.

My feet ache.

I settle myself on the sofa in the sitting room with the book.

And I wait.

Still Dad doesn't come.

I distract myself with doodles and drawings in the sketchbook.

I try writing a story with pictures, for Kelda. I draw her with her funny skirt and boots. I make up adventures for her, and make it silly so she'll laugh. We had such beautiful books when I was little. It's Dad's job, illustrating picture books.

For dinner I make a sort of soup, with stuff from the remaining tins. I put more wood on the stove. I light the candle lanterns with a twist of paper lit from the stove. I put one lantern in the window, to shine the way home.

Still Dad doesn't come.

I leave the doors unlocked in case he arrives in the middle of the night.

I lie awake in bed for hours. It starts to rain, heavy, drenching rain that batters the windows. The river will be rising. How much rain does it take before the river floods? How high does the water come? What if the road gets washed away?

What if Dad doesn't come back?

In the pit of my stomach, fear uncurls.

Thirteen

I wake, heart thudding. What was that?

I lie dead still, straining to hear.

The light at the window is pale grey. It must be very early morning. There's the silence that comes after sudden unexpected noise, and then the first flutey notes of birdsong.

Did I *imagine* the sound? Shouts, the barking of a dog. Was it part of a dream?

I'm fully awake now. I pull on clothes, go to the window, hide half behind the curtain so I can check outside without being seen. Nothing. I creep to the front windows, pull back the curtain enough so I can see the line of the road. Nothing there, either, but my heart's still thudding, as if my animal body *knows* there's something dangerous out there. *Someone.*

The house doors are unlocked, in case Dad arrived in the night.

I run downstairs to the kitchen and slide the big iron bolt across the back door. I run down the hall to the front door and do the same.

Voices echo from the fells opposite. Three figures come down over the ridge, dark silhouettes against the sky.

Who are they?

Why are they here?

I shrink back from the window. Where can I hide? What if they try to get into the house?

What's happened to Dad?

I remember what Rowan said about the men who came and cleared out the houses, took away the sick people and rounded up the children. Already I'm imagining a knock at the door, the sound of splintering wood as they bash it down . . . the smash of window glass . . .

Now I can hear different voices rise and fall, discussing something.

The dog growls.

They're very close to the house.

I crawl across the hall and into the small bathroom. It's the one room with a lock on the door and no window. I sit on the wooden seat, my heart banging in my chest.

Why isn't Dad back?

It goes quiet.

I wait, and listen, and finally I hear footsteps again, and muffled voices. But the sounds get fainter, the footsteps are moving away.

At last I dare to come out of the bathroom and peer through the window. There's no sign of anyone.

Kelda and Rowan! I have to warn them!

I shove on my boots and warm coat. I unbolt the back door with trembling hands as quietly as I can. I lock it after me with the heavy metal key. I hide the key on the nail in the shed where Dad can find it.

And I run.

I slip down the path to the river and cross the bridge. Clamber up the other side, run through the woods. It feels safer under the trees: I'm hidden from view. There's faint comfort in the familiar sounds of birdsong and water. But soon I'm through the copse. Up on the fell, the path is totally exposed. It's beginning to rain. The path ahead disappears into low cloud.

I stop at the ruined house to catch my breath.

The fox springs up in surprise. There's a moment when we look right at each other before it slips away through a gap in the wall. I don't know which of us is more startled. It must have been sleeping in the house. Kelda's fox. It streaks away along the ridge and disappears into the bracken.

I cross the rickety bridge over Swinner Gill. The water is flowing fast, tumbling down the hillside to join the river. The ridge path is narrow and slippery in the rain so I have to slow down.

Am I in time?

I run the last section down from the high fell to the field and the barn, slipping and sliding through the wet grass.

Rowan comes out of the doorway to the barn. 'Whatever's the matter?'

I fling myself at him. 'Get inside! Where's Kelda?'

I push him back into the barn. 'There are people coming this way. Quick! You have to hide!'

Rowan takes a deep breath. 'What?'

'I ran the whole way. They could be here any minute.'

He narrows his eyes. 'What's your dad gone and said?'

'Nothing!'

'Did you tell him about us?'

'No!' I'm practically crying. 'Of course not. I promised, didn't I?'

'Did they see you?'

'No, I hid in the house till they'd gone. I ran all the way here to warn you and Kelda. Where is she?'

'She's still sleeping. It's OK. Calm down.'

'Rowan, it's not OK. What if they see smoke from the fire? Or the patch you've been digging? Or the chickens . . .'

'I haven't let the chickens out yet. The fox was lurking about, earlier.' Rowan frowns. 'I'll join Kelda in the hayloft. Keep her quiet.'

'Be quick,' I whisper. 'And put out the fire.'

'Are you crazy? We can't let the fire go out.'

Everything takes so long. He clambers over the wooden partition, drops down the other side with a thud. The hens squawk.

He says something to Kelda, and she replies in a small, sleepy voice.

'Now we must be very, very quiet,' he tells her. 'Like when we play hide-and-seek.'

'Why?' she says. 'I want to see Isabella!'

Rowan shushes her again. 'Soon,' he says.

I wriggle into the darkness in the corner of the room, my back against the barn wall. There are chinks of light, gaps between the stones I can peer through. I hear the *croak croak* of a raven flying over the field. The rustle of hay as Rowan or Kelda shifts position in the loft. Nothing for a while. And then comes the faint sound of voices, and the excited bark of the dog.

Fourteen

Rowan sings softly to Kelda. I know he's trying to keep her calm and quiet, but it makes me nervous. Fragments of the song drift over from the hayloft . . . the sad words of an old ballad about a mother and a child. Doesn't he know anything more cheerful?

Everything sounds too loud: the song, the clucking chickens, Kelda's attempts at whispering. Even my own breath, my beating heart.

The dog barks. And suddenly there are shouting voices. The dog's coming this way, running up the field. Someone calls and whistles to it but it races on up. It briefly stops barking, sniffs in circles around the field, tail wagging, then takes off again, following a scent. Hunting.

Rowan muffles Kelda's scream.

I shift my position.

The dog is chasing something.

A flash of orange in the bracken.

The young fox.

Rowan's voice. 'The fox knows where to hide. She'll go to earth.'

'Let me GO!' Kelda, furious. 'You don't CARE! You hate my fox.'

'Ouch! You bit me!'

'Sssh!' I whisper.

The dog is still running over the fell, circling, nose to the ground. The fox has disappeared.

The dog seems unsure what to do. It stops running. It has one last go at finding the scent of the fox, tracks back and forth through the dry bracken, then gives up. It lopes across the fell, over the next field and races down towards the river after the people.

I don't see their faces, just their backs.

There are three of them.

And one of them looks small enough to be a child.

'Did you see? Rowan? They weren't soldiers! Not scary people! More like a family. Shall I run after them? Say hello. They might have seen Dad!'

Rowan and Kelda climb down from the hayloft.

Rowan stares from the doorway. The people have disappeared over the hill.

Why isn't he more excited?

I babble on. 'Perhaps they're living in a barn like you and Kelda. Maybe there are other children who survived the sickness and hid.'

'We'd know. We'd have seen them.'

'Not if they wanted to stay hidden.'

He frowns. 'So why would they be here now, in broad daylight? With a noisy, pestering dog?'

'I don't know. But wouldn't it be wonderful, to have more people near? Let's go after them. Talk to them, at least. Find out who they are. Where they're from.'

'And risk everything? Are you mad?'

Rowan's angry.

Doesn't he want there to be anyone else?

But I know that *angry* sometimes means *frightened*. He's scared of what it means. He needs time to think about it all. So I don't say anything more. Not yet.

The kittens have grown since I last saw them. Their eyes are open, and their claws and teeth are as sharp as needles. The mother cat hisses when I pick one up. I smooth its soft fur and put it back down. She licks it all over to rid it of my touch and smell.

Kelda sits close to me, her small hand in mine. She's subdued, unusually quiet. Rowan puts wood on the fire and takes a pan to fetch water from the well.

'It's OK,' I tell Kelda. 'We're all perfectly safe.' I tell her I saw her little fox inside the ruined house. 'It sleeps there,' I say.

She nods. 'I know. Don't tell Rowan, but sometimes I leave food there for her.' She looks at me. 'That horrible dog chased her.'

'Yes, but the fox got away. The dog didn't catch her. Your fox is much cleverer than a barky dog.'

Breakfast is some kind of weird soup with leaves and broth, but I'm so hungry I eat it all. Rowan asks me about Dad.

'He said he'd be back yesterday. I don't know why he isn't back. I'm really worried about him.'

Rowan's face softens at last. 'He's been delayed,

that's all. Maybe he's waiting for supplies to arrive at the shop. Or maybe he had to go on somewhere else, to a bigger town. All the way to the coast, even, to the port. That would take a long time on foot.'

'What if he's hurt himself?'

He shakes his head. 'No point thinking like that. Stay here with us, if you want. Help with seed planting today. Later, I'll show you how to set a snare for fresh meat.'

He goes outside. 'Kelda?' he calls.

He calls her name again. He goes round to the hayloft. He comes back in. 'Where did she go? Did you see?'

'No.' We scan the field, and the fells. Nothing moves except a pair of buzzards circling high above the hill. The rain has stopped and the sky is clearing to pale blue.

'She must have wandered off when we were talking,' I say. 'She was worried about the fox. Perhaps she went to look for it.'

Rowan sighs. 'She'll not go far. We'll get on faster without her.' He shows me how to plant seed potatoes, spacing them out in rows. We sow peas next. It's satisfying seeing the line of wizened old peas and covering them with fresh soil and watering them from the well, imagining the fresh pea shoots growing. The pigeons love peas too, Rowan says. But pigeon meat makes a tasty stew so it balances out. He shows me the new young nettle leaves growing in the field. 'They're good for you,' he says. 'You can make soup. And dry them for tea. Dried heather flowers make good tea, too.'

He says nothing about the people and the dog.

In my mind I make up different versions of who they are, and where they're from, and what they were doing in our valley. I make up happy endings for everybody. Like wishes, when you blow out candles on a birthday cake, or see a rainbow or a shooting star.

I stretch out my aching spine. 'Kelda's probably at the ruined house,' I say. 'Shall I go and find her?'

'She'll be back when she's hungry. I can't be chasing after her all the time.'

But she doesn't come back, not even when it's lunchtime.

I leave Rowan to his digging and make my way home.

I try to keep busy, to stop myself worrying about

Dad. I draw in my sketchbook: the fox, and the dog, and the three people.

I start another letter to Marta. I tell her about what happened this morning.

Maybe there are more children in the valley, I write. Rowan was weird about the people we saw. But I think it would be good; they could be friends. We could help each other. Maybe they know something about my dad.

I don't understand why Rowan won't talk about things.

Oh Marta if only you were here. I miss you so much.

xxxxxxxxxxxxxx

Dusk falls. I light the candles in the lanterns. I wait. Every small noise makes me jump. I'm on full alert.

Finally, *finally*, I hear the squeak of the front gate being pushed open. Relief floods through me. At last!

I run from the living room to open the front door for him.

'OH!'

Not Dad, but Rowan.

Fifteen

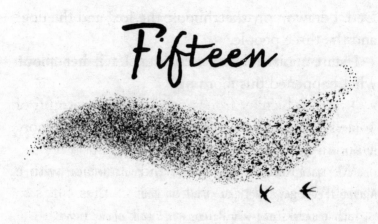

He's clutching a bundle of wet clothes in his arms, he's soaked through, he looks terrified.

'Why—what are you doing here? Rowan—?'

It's not a bundle of clothes. He's holding Kelda, crumpled and limp in his arms. Dripping wet.

'What—*oh no*!'

'She was in the river.' Rowan staggers inside. 'She nearly drowned. I didn't know what to do. Help me—'

She's so pale I think for a horrible second that she's actually dead.

Rowan gabbles at me. 'It's my fault, I should have looked for her earlier, she was in the river, she would

have been swept under only her clothes got caught
on a tree—'

'Bring her into the kitchen. It's the warmest place.
Lie her on the couch.'

I fetch a blanket from upstairs, and an armful of
towels. I fill the kettle and set it to heat. I put more
wood in the stove.

We rub Kelda's hair and hands and face with a
towel. We gently peel off her wet clothes. She's so
small and skinny I could cry. We dry her with the
towels and wrap her in the dry blanket, and little by
little, colour comes back into her skin. Her eyes are
still tight shut.

I rest my hand on her chest, to feel it rise and fall
with each breath.

'How much water did she swallow?' I ask.

'Loads, but I got most of it out of her, I think. She
coughed and sicked it up once I'd got her out on the
riverbank.'

'You should take your wet clothes off, too,' I say.
He's in shock.

'Grab one of the towels. My grandpa's old
clothes are still hanging in a wardrobe upstairs.
The room above this one, at the top of the stairs.

Help yourself. You're shaking with cold. I'll watch Kelda.'

I sit close to warm her with the heat from my own body. I rub her hands and feet very gently. I try to remember the lessons we had at school about first aid. *Keep warm. Recovery position. Check airways.* I can see Kelda's breathing. Maybe she injured herself when she fell . . . I find bruises, scratches on her arms, and her left ankle is swollen and bruised. There's a bump on her head.

She whimpers, and I lean in close. I talk softly to her. 'It's OK, Kelda. You're safe now. You're in my house. Isabella's. Rowan's here too. We're looking after you.'

Rowan comes back into the kitchen. He's wearing a baggy woollen jumper and brown cord trousers with the legs rolled up. He looks different in clean clothes with his hair smoothed down.

'She's coming round. Did she hit her head? Tell me what happened.'

I make us tea. Rowan sits with Kelda's head on his lap. He strokes her hair back from her face. He looks at her with such love and tenderness and sorrow.

'It wasn't your fault,' I say gently.

He doesn't know how long she was in the water. He only went to look for her when it was starting to get dark and she hadn't come home. He guesses she went looking for the fox, and somehow slipped and fell in the river.

'The river's in spate,' he says. 'All that rain last night. She wouldn't be able to get out with the floodwater pushing her along. The banks are too steep and slippery. She'd have been swept even further if that tree hadn't been there, jammed into the bank.'

He begins to weep: the silent, stifled sobs of someone who has not cried for a very long time. Who has held everything together, alone, for much too long. Tears that have been buried deep.

He'll be embarrassed that I've seen him like this. But he doesn't need to be. I've seen my dad cry. It doesn't mean you're not strong. It's OK to be terrified that your sister could so easily have drowned.

I put more wood in the stove.

He stops shaking. He drinks the tea. He looks around the kitchen as if he's taking it in for the first time.

Kelda warms up at last. She's still trembling, but her hands and feet are no longer icy. She opens her eyes.

'I fell,' she says. 'Over and over and tumbling down. And then it went dark. My head hurts,' she says.

Rowan rests his hands on her head. 'You must have hit it very hard,' he says. 'There's a lump like an egg.'

She feels it with her own hand, and then she starts to cry.

It's as if her body is waking up to the pain, and it's only now she knows she's safe that she can show us how frightened she actually was.

Rowan holds her close. I stroke her feet. All the time, I'm trying to listen to her breathing, because I'm remembering what we were taught about the danger of water in the lungs, and the risk of pneumonia, and the need to get help. But there's no ambulance out here, no hospital, no doctor, no phone even. There's no one but Rowan and me.

Her chest rises and falls. Her breathing sounds steady to me, once she's stopped crying. But I don't really know.

'Should we put her to bed?' I say to Rowan. 'I think she needs to be kept dry and warm. You'll both have to stay here tonight, and maybe longer.'

He's torn between wanting to escape back to his barn, and the need to care for his sister.

'What if your dad comes back?'

'It's dark,' I say. 'I don't think he will now, not tonight. And if he does, I'll explain, and make him promise not to tell anyone. He'll understand. Really he will. He'll help us.'

We're all dropping with tiredness. I show Rowan where he and Kelda can sleep tonight, and help him tuck her into bed.

She still hasn't properly woken up. She opens her eyes briefly, but I'm not sure she knows where she is or why.

'I'll stay beside her,' Rowan says.

I pause in the bedroom doorway. 'I'm glad you brought her here.'

A white moth blunders around the candle on the table. I watch it fly perilously close to the flame. There's a brief flutter and then *Snap!* The moth burns up. A life extinguished.

Sixteen

I wake in the night with a start. Someone's wandering about. The stairs creak under their tread. My heart lurches with hope: *Dad's home?* And then I remember Rowan. I climb out of bed and open my door a crack.

The faintest hint of light and shadow. I slip out of my room onto the landing. There's the click of the key turning in the back door, and a soft thud as someone shoves the door when it sticks on the step.

Across the landing, the door to Rowan and Kelda's room is ajar. I can make out her sleeping form in the bed, and the pushed-back bedding where Rowan's

got out. So it's him, downstairs. I listen, to make sure
Kelda's breathing OK. I go back to bed, but I can't
sleep. Not till I hear him come back up. I wait and
wait and I still don't hear him.

Early morning. Grey light at the window. Someone
singing to herself. Coughing. Singing again.

I pad across the landing.

Kelda's sitting up in bed, her messy hair a bird's
nest against the pillow.

'You're awake!'

She waves. 'Awake awake awake!' she crows.
'Rowan's gone to feed the fire and let out the
chickens.' She coughs again.

Ah.

'Will he come back?'

'Of course!'

She smiles. 'I had the loveliest sleep in this soft
lovely bed in this lovely lovely house!'

'That's a lot of lovelies!' I say.

She stretches out her arms against the pillows.
'Sooooooo soft.'

'How do you feel this morning? How's your
head?'

'Not so achey.'

'Good.'

'But it hurts here.' She rests her hand on her chest. She does a little cough, to demonstrate.

'Well, that's why you should stay warm and cosy in bed today,' I say. 'Your body needs a rest so it can get completely better. So you stay here, and I'll get breakfast.'

The air is warmer this morning. The rain has stopped. I fill the kettle with spring water. The garden is full of birdsong. The robin is back, watching me from its perch on the wall. The blackbird calls from the apple tree. Surely Dad will be back today. And maybe Mum and Gabriella will be with him—perhaps he walked all the way to the station, and waited for them, to bring them here.

They will meet Kelda and Rowan, because we can't move Kelda yet, and I won't have to keep them secret any more and it will be much better like that . . .

I take Kelda a cup of nettle tea and the last packet of crackers. The dry biscuits make her cough.

She pushes them away. 'I want Rowan,' she croaks. She coughs.

'I know. I expect he'll be here soon. Try to drink the tea. It will help your cough.'

She's pale. Her head feels clammy against my cool hand. I try to soothe her. She's restless and feverish.

I fetch my sketchbook to show her my drawings and take her mind off being ill.

She likes the birds—the dipper and the flock of fieldfares. She turns the page. 'That's me!'

I read her the silly story I made up about her adventures.

'Again!'

I read it over and over.

She wants more stories.

I tell her about my life back home, and she leans in close to listen. She keeps coughing. She watches my face all the time while I describe our flat, and the streets and squares, full of life and noise and people.

I tell her about hot sunshine, and ice cream. 'You know when water freezes and makes ice on puddles? Imagine frozen milk that tastes of sweet berries.'

I tell her about the stationery shop, and school, and about Marta. My voice cracks when I talk about Marta. 'I've known her my whole life. Since we were babies. Our mums were in the same hospital ward.'

Kelda looks at me. 'Hospital?' she asks.

I take a deep breath. 'A special place to look after people who are sick, with doctors and nurses to make them better with medicines and operations and it's very clean and shiny and some mums have their babies there or you can have a baby at home . . .'

'I know about having babies,' Kelda says. 'Kitten babies born at home.'

She tugs my arm. 'Isabella? What's wrong?'

I wipe my eyes on my sleeve. 'Just thinking about Mum and Marta and home.' I try to smile for her, but the tears keep coming.

For Marta.

For Mamma.

For me.

I'm worried about Kelda. She needs a hospital, and doctors, and people to look after her who know what to do.

My whole life, I've been surrounded by people. Not just family and friends but everyone in our neighbourhood. Ilaria, the lady who lives below us, and the Marinelli family across the street, and Alessandro and Carlo who run the grocery shop on the corner. Irene and Giulia and all the people Mum works with at the publishing house, and the funny man who comes to the square at dusk on Saturday nights to play the accordion and dance a strange dance with balloons, like someone from the circus, candles arranged around his square of red cloth on the cobbled street.

In my old life I was hardly ever alone.

I never had to decide anything by myself.

I had no responsibilities.

How can I explain any of this to Kelda? She knows nothing about the world. Knows nothing about all the things missing from her life. All she has is one brother, and the memory of parents caught in a single faded photograph.

She falls asleep against me.

I watch her chest rise and fall with each noisy breath. She coughs and coughs but she doesn't wake up.

Mamma used to tell Dad that a good night's sleep is important for healing. *But you shouldn't stay in bed all day, Daniel. That does you no good. Get out into the world. Get out of your own head.*

Kelda sleeps and sleeps. It's what she needs. She's *healing*, I tell myself. I go downstairs but it's hard to concentrate on anything. What if she's getting sicker? Her coughing echoes through the house. I check on her all through the day. When she wakes briefly, I make her sip water. She doesn't speak.

She's getting worse.

'At last!' I say, when Rowan finally comes to the door. 'I'm worried. She's getting sicker.'

I follow him up the stairs.

'Kelda!'

She doesn't wake.

He studies her face, lifts her hand and tucks it under the blanket. He rests his hand on her forehead. He listens to her ragged breathing.

'Is it a fever?' I ask. 'What should we do?'

'Let her sleep. She's tough, she'll be OK.'

'Is there something we could give her? Medicine or something?'

'Like what?'

'I don't know. A plant remedy. Herbs. There must be something we can do. I'm scared for her.'

I can tell he's afraid, too. But he won't admit it. Won't look at me. He's on edge the whole time he's in the house.

He stands up. 'I can carry her back to the barn if you don't want her here.'

'Don't be stupid. You can't move her when she's so sick! I know she's little, but she's too heavy for you to carry her all that way.'

'I carried her before, from the river.'

'I'll look after her. But why can't you be here, too? She's your sister!'

'There are the hens, and the fire has to be kept alight. I'll be back in the morning.'

He clatters back downstairs. The back door clicks shut.

Hopeless.

So it's just Kelda and me, now. I pull the curtains to keep out the blank darkness.

I settle down on the chair next to the bed.

Watch and wait.

Dad doesn't come back.

I go downstairs to put more wood on the stove. I light a candle and bring it back to the bedroom.

I'm so sleepy I can hardly think. But I daren't

leave Kelda. Her breathing is unsteady. She takes big, rasping breaths. I shift her higher onto the stack of pillows, to make it easier to breathe.

I lean over her. Whisper, 'I'm here, Kelda. You're safe. You'll be better soon.' Soothing words like Dad used to say when I was little and sick.

But I was never this sick. Might she die?

I doze in the half-light. The candle flame flickers in the draught.

I jerk awake. The room is in total darkness.

Something's changed. I know it with my whole body.

I put my hand on Kelda's head. She's burning hot.

I run downstairs and outside to the spring to fetch more water. There's a bright silver half-moon and hundreds of stars. I take in big gulps of the cold, clean air. The sky is immense, a vast canopy. A fox barks.

I go back inside with the bowl of spring water.

I light the candle from the stove and take it carefully back upstairs.

I dip the edge of a towel in the cold water and wipe Kelda's head and neck and hands. She's mumbling words, but nothing makes any sense. *Delirious.* I've seen it on films, but never in real life before.

Over and over I bathe Kelda's face and forehead, her arms and hands.

Three times I have to go back to the spring to refill the bowl with cold water.

Hours pass, the candle burns lower.
I sink back into deep sleep.

Seventeen

Light seeps through the thin curtains.

Why is it so silent?

I straighten up. My neck and back are stiff from a night slumped half in the chair, half over the bed.

I daren't look.

And then I do.

Kelda lies on her side, face away from me.

Her body moves gently with each breath. She's alive. Sleeping.

I reach over and touch her forehead. Hot, but not burning hot. Her face is very pale.

And she's alive.

Three black and white magpies fly off as I open the back door and step into the garden. The grass is damp with dew. I fill the kettle from the spring. My hands shake as I lift the little cup on the string. The intense fear from last night floods through my whole body.

I sit on the back step to drink nettle tea.

The stove needs more fuel.

I open the shed door. A spider dangles on a long string. There's the piney smell of freshly cut wood; a neat stack of logs that wasn't there yesterday.

From Rowan, of course. His way of showing he cares about his sister. But I'm still angry that he left me to do it all alone.

I take a glass of water up to Kelda but she's fast asleep. A different kind of sleep from yesterday: calm and restful. I watch her. She'll be OK on her own for a while. She's going to get better. She is, she is, I tell myself. She has to.

I rummage in the larder for something to eat and find one last tin of beans. I eat half the contents, cold, straight from the tin, sitting on the back doorstep. The granite is cold under my legs. The chill seeps through my whole body but I stay sitting there, too tired and lazy to move. The sun moves higher, until it's shining right on my face, and the first warmth spreads into my bones.

Here's Rowan, at last. Dark worry circles under his eyes. Pale.

I thought I was going to yell and be furious with him. Instead, I tell him she seems a bit better, now. 'Sleeping.'

'But it was awful,' I say. 'You should have stayed. I thought she might die in the night.'

His eyes widen in alarm.

'She came through it. The fever went down.'

'Sorry,' he mumbles.

'You should go up and see her.'

He nods.

'Brought you these.' He holds out a hessian sack.

'What's that?'

He unties the string around the top and out flutter two squawking brown hens. 'Now you'll have your own eggs.'

'Thank you.'

Rowan explains how to look after them—we

don't have chicken food but the hens will find grubs and caterpillars and insects in the garden, and as long as they have fresh water and I shut them up at night, they'll be fine. Their poo will fertilise the soil. We can make a space for them in a corner of the woodshed.

'Thanks for the logs,' I say.

I tell him about the night. 'She had a fever. High temperature. She was delirious. And coughing, but not properly waking up. She was really sick.

'Her cough's not so bad this morning. And she's calm, sleeping.'

'I'm sorry, I should have stayed. I'll go and see her now.'

The hens get bolder, exploring further into the wild garden. They stay close to each other, clucking and making funny soft sounds in their throats, like talking. Their big, scaly feet scratch the ground. They rake dust bowls in patches of dry earth.

I sit quietly and they come and explore me too. I pick one up and feel its quick-beating heart under the soft feathers. She has a patch of almost white feathers under her chin. 'I will call you Bianca. And your sister can be Sylvie. Now settle yourselves in your new home. I'm going inside.'

Kelda's awake.

I hover in the doorway. Rowan's sitting very close to her, his hand on her cheek. She looks pale and exhausted. She coughs. She doesn't see me.

I go back downstairs.I run down to the river, across the bridge, drop a stick in to see how fast the current is. The water's still high after all the rain. Perhaps there are floods further down the valley. Perhaps Dad has had to wait for the water to go down. *He'll be back soon*, I tell myself. *He will.*

I climb up to the ruined house and sit in the empty rooms. Loneliness washes over me. What if he never comes? What if something bad has happened to him, and to Mum and Gabriella? What if this is all there ever is? Scraping together a kind of life in this empty valley, with just Rowan and Kelda and a couple of hens for company. It isn't enough. I couldn't bear it.

I cry miserable, hot tears, and then I make myself stop.

I fish my sketchbook out of my pocket and begin

to draw. I force myself to focus on something else, something outside myself.

Landscapes are hard. The perspective, what to put in, what to leave out. How to draw leaves on a tree. Clouds. I've looked at the view from here so many times, and yet when I try to draw it, it's as if I haven't paid any attention to it before. The shape of the fells. The winding river far below. The different colours of a hillside. And what's the point in trying to draw it at all? What's the point of anything, when it can all be snatched away in an instant?

Kelda could have died. And what's happened to Marta?

I give up. I trail back to the house.

The hens are making a fuss about something. I go over to see what they're doing.

Sylvie has laid an egg! A small, pointed, thin-shelled egg.

It's warm in my hand. The first one. A thing of wonder!

I take it to show Kelda.

She's still awake, sitting up in bed, talking to Rowan. She's telling him the stories I told her, about my life back home.

He's listening intently, saying nothing.

Does he hate me for telling his sister about all these things that she doesn't have, won't ever have?

I tiptoe away again. I don't show her the freshly laid egg. It's only special to me because it's my very first one. She must have collected new-laid eggs a hundred times.

Eighteen

Dear Marta,

Dad still hasn't come back. I am seriously worried something terrible has happened because he would never stay away so long on purpose. What do you think I should I do, Marta? Go and look for him? Just wait? It is almost unbearable.

I wish you could write to me or phone or best of all I could see you. It seems ages since we said goodbye, the day of the explosions. I've written to you every day. I miss you so much.

Kelda is still here. I thought Rowan might resent the way Kelda and I are getting closer, spending so much time together. I expected him to be angry about the things I'm showing her. Maybe he is, a bit. But he brought me two scrawny hens (alive ones), to say thank you for looking after her. It means we now have our own food supply (eggs). They run up making soft clucky sounds when they see me. It reminds me of being at Nonna's. I have to shut them in the shed at night so the fox can't get them. This morning Rowan brought a rabbit he'd snared (skinned and chopped up already, you will be pleased to know), so I can make stew. I am learning which plants are OK for eating (nettle tops, dandelion, sorrel, new beech and hawthorn leaves, fat-hen, chickweed, hop, shepherd's purse). I found clumps of wild mint growing in the garden.

Kelda being so ill was the scariest thing ever. I thought she might actually die. We have no medicines and there is no one to help. Anyway, now she's feeling better she wants to know everything about my old life. I have decided I am going to teach her to read and write while she is here. I have told her all about you—

'Isabella! Where are you?' Kelda's voice drifts downstairs.

'Coming!' I call back.

'I need a wee!'

I help her out of bed and downstairs and out to the ancient loo in the shed.

We stay outside for a while to enjoy the sun on our faces and to watch the happy hens scratch and peck. Kelda looks happier, too. Soon she'll be strong enough to run and play outside again. She manages the walk back inside by herself, and we settle at the dining room table to draw picture and tell stories.

She loves the map and the photos on the walls. I show her how to find the barn and this house on the map, and the ruined house where her fox sleeps. I spell out the names. I write them in the sketchbook and she traces the letters as we say the words aloud.

Swallow Fell. I'd thought it was because of swallows, the birds. But Rowan explained about *swallow holes*, where a stream gets swallowed up into the underlying limestone rock. The fells are riddled with them. You have to be careful because sometimes the water bores through and makes the rock collapse. You could fall in.

Kelda tries to draw her own map but she gets frustrated and scribbles over all the lines in thick orange pen. She peers at the old photos on the walls.

'That one is my Grandma Frieda,' I tell her. 'She lived in this house.'

'She's a little girl, not a grandma,' Kelda says.

'Everyone was a child, and before that a baby, before they grew up!'

Kelda laughs, as if it's the funniest thought. 'I was a tiny baby and so was Rowan! And you!'

I draw us as babies. A row of babies. Kelda colours us in. I draw the kittens. She colours them very carefully, tabby and black and white.

'Soon there will be baby birds everywhere.' I draw some nests with chicks inside.

'Where was I before I was a baby?' Kelda asks.

'You were growing inside your mum.'

'Before that?'

I laugh. 'Nowhere,' I say. 'Nowhere and nothing.'

I open my sketchbook. 'Now, we're going to practise reading.'

I point at the story words I've written for Kelda, and say them out loud. She looks, and points, and says them after me. She's a quick learner. She loves to do new things. Her mind is wide open to everything.

And that's how our days go on. Slow, and simple, and sometimes almost happy.

The dark shadows gather at night, as soon as Kelda is asleep and I am alone again. In the darkness, my mind whirls and spirals out of control. My body aches with loneliness and longing.

Dad. Mamma. Gabriella. Marta.

Nineteen

The worry about Dad is a stone in my stomach. I carry it everywhere with me. It's there when I get into bed, and when I jolt awake in the middle of the night, my heart hammering. It's there when I wake up first thing in the morning. It has become part of me. This is how I live now.

We have days of bright, brilliant sunshine and sudden downpours of rain. Clouds scud across the pale blue sky. I call to Kelda to come and see a massive rainbow arching the valley, and she laughs at my excitement. Everything seems so bright and shiny after the sodden grey days that went before. Tight buds uncurl and burst into bright new leaves.

The pale green haze of the woodland becomes solid green. We draw the things we see each day, a picture diary of our lives.

We find a small blue eggshell under the apple tree. I hold it in my cupped hand: so delicate and beautiful. 'See how lovely it is!'

'The colour of sky!' Kelda says.

We look for a nest in the tree above.

There it is! A neat bowl woven from twigs and grass and feather wedged in a fork on a branch. In a few days' time we'll hear the cheeping of baby birds, and watch the parent birds flying to and fro with worms and bugs for the babies.

Dear Marta,

The bank near the waterfall is smothered in pale yellow flowers set in rosettes of leaves—prim roses, Kelda calls them. The river has a different voice: lighter and happier as it flows over the stones and races under the bridge.

The birds sing louder. They wake me earlier each morning. Everything is fresh and hopeful. Kelda's voice is a new song filling the house.

Our days have a new pattern. I let out the hens first thing. After breakfast we do our reading and writing at the table.

We draw and paint and make up stories. We've used up most of Dad's paints.

I haven't given up, I know something important must be keeping him away, that he'd never choose to stay so long. He will come back soon. I have to be patient.

Patience is something I am learning from Rowan.

He turns up at lunchtime, most days. He brings meat or something he's made. We chop wood together for the stove, or clear more of the garden. He brought bean seedlings for me to plant out in the patch we've dug and weeded. We play with Kelda her made-up games. Sometimes he doesn't come till late afternoon, and Kelda sits on the front step to watch and wait for him. She's better, stronger.

Do you think of me, Marta? I miss you so much!

Your loving friend,

Isabella

Late afternoon. I'm filling the hens' water bowl in the garden, when I hear an unfamiliar *tick–tick–tick*. A sound I recognize from the old days but can't quite place.

Rowan appears around the side of the house. He's pushing a bike. A very old, rusty bike with funny handlebars and a leather seat, but nonetheless a bike that works.

'Wow!' I say.

He grins.

'That's amazing! Where did you find it?'

'A shed, two villages down the valley.' He looks properly pleased with himself.

Each day without Kelda, he tells me, he's been going further, exploring the empty villages. The bike is the best thing ever. A bike means freedom to travel.

We watch Kelda, crouched at the edge of the vegetable patch, talking to the hens.

'She's well enough now to go back home with you,' I say.

Rowan doesn't answer. He pushes the bike to one of the sheds and leans it there. He walks slowly back to me carrying an old sack. He holds it out. 'Dinner. I'll put it in the kitchen.'

I follow him inside. 'What is it?'

'Fish.'

'No, I mean what is bothering you? What's the matter?'

'Nothing.'

'Yes, there is. I can always tell, Rowan!'

'Kelda.'

'What about her?'

'She's happy here,' he finally says. 'She's happier living with you than with me.'

'That's not true!'

'It is. I've watched her. It's obvious. She likes living in a proper house, and the things you do with her. You're more fun than me. I don't blame her.'

'Yes, but you're her brother. Her home will always be with you.'

He fiddles with the edge of the bag. He won't look at me.

'It's easier without her, at the barn,' he mumbles.

I get it.

He likes his new freedom. It's a relief not having to look after Kelda. He wants more of it.

'So?' I finally say.

He shrugs. 'I don't know . . . I thought you liked having her. She could stay here. And if your dad comes back—'

'When, not if.'

'Maybe he would, too.'

'I do like having her here. Dad will love her, when he gets to meet her. But you would miss her terribly. You'd be totally alone. Anyway, she'd miss you. She waits for you every day. She loves you.'

Rowan doesn't answer. He gets the fish out of the bag, takes his knife from his belt and starts to clean out the fish guts. He leaves the cleaned fish on the table ready for cooking, and scrapes the guts and head and stuff back into the bag. He wipes the knife clean.

He looks up. 'There's something else,' he says.

'What?'

'Yesterday I cycled a long way down the valley. Saw smoke in the distance. I reckon someone's living in the old mine house above the village where the school used to be.'

'Those people with the dog! I bet it's them.'

'I'm going to go and see. I've decided.'

I stare at him. It's what I said we should do, when we first saw them. But . . .

I swallow hard.

'Don't leave without Kelda and me. All three of us should go together.'

He goes quiet.

'How is that even possible?' he says, eventually. 'Three people, one bike. It's much too far for Kelda.'

'We could walk, and push her on the bike. Or take it in turns, or something.'

He still doesn't say anything.

'We need to stick together,' I say. 'You can't just go off and leave Kelda with me. She's YOUR sister. It's not fair!'

'Fair? When was anything ever *fair*?'

For a moment I'm too angry to speak. Then I blurt it all out.

'Supposing you don't come back? Supposing it's not safe? Supposing something happens to you? And Kelda and I are left totally alone struggling to survive here for EVER? Have you thought of that? Of course not. You just do what YOU want!'

I storm upstairs. I slam all the doors. I lie on my bed and let angry hot tears trickle down my face and onto the pillow.

It's what I used to do when I was little. I know it's childish of me. I'd lie on my bed, and eventually Dad would come into my room, and sit on the bed beside me, and talk softly to me, and let me cry, and then he'd help me up and we'd go back to the dinner table together. It was always mealtimes, for some reason. And I can't even remember what made me so cross, back then. Back in that old life.

No one comes to rescue me from myself now, of

course. Not even Kelda, who so often understands when I'm sad or upset.

Eventually I go back downstairs.

Rowan's in the kitchen, cooking the fish.

Kelda's sitting on the table with her feet on a chair, chatting to him.

I slip into the dining room and open my notebook and start writing.

Dear Marta,

But that's all I write. I can't find the words any more. For the first time, it seems utterly pointless to write a letter that I can't post.

I have a whole fat bundle of letters.

Marta hasn't read any of them.

I'm stupid.

I go back to the kitchen and flump down at the table.

Rowan has cooked the fish with wild thyme and young nettle tops. He ladles some into a bowl for me.

It tastes delicious but I don't tell him that. I don't say anything at all. Kelda talks non-stop about a new game she's made up.

After dinner, I don't join in the game. I wander out to the garden and sit on the wall by myself.

When it begins to get dark, I shoo the two hens into the barn for the night.

Rowan and Kelda come outside.

'I'm off home,' Rowan announces.

'Night night. See you tomorrow,' Kelda says. She hugs him.

He fetches the bike from the shed.

Kelda comes over and puts her hand in mine.

We watch him go.

Tick-tick-tick.

Twenty

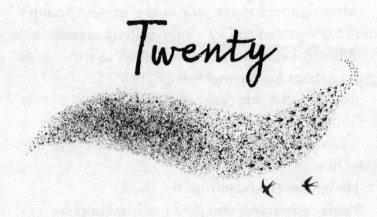

The next morning, I go down to the shed to let out our two hens.

SIX hens and one angry cockerel run squawking past me and out through the open door. Rowan must have brought them over while Kelda and I were still asleep. He wants us to look after them. And I know what that means. He's gone; cycled away without a word. Left me to explain to Kelda what he's doing.

But she doesn't seem to mind.

The following morning, the young fox is curled up on a sun-warmed stone just beyond the garden wall.

'She's followed me here,' Kelda says. 'She's happy she's found me!'

'She's found where the hens are, more likely.'

The fox lifts her head at the sound of our voices. She springs up and lopes away from the garden towards the field.

Kelda runs after her.

'You've got bare feet! Get dressed first!' I call after her, but she takes no notice.

I fill the hens' water bowl from the spring. I hunker down on the old wall and watch them scratch and peck and drink. Kelda said the cockerel guards the hens and will chase the fox away if it comes too close. Is she right? I've no idea. But I do know we need those hens; their eggs keep us alive.

The pea and bean seedlings are growing taller. The parent robins fly back and forth to the nest in the ivy on the shed. There's a constant *cheep cheep* from the blackbird chicks in their nest in the apple tree. Pink buds on the bare twigs mean flowers and later fruit. That's almost all I think of now: what can we eat? We pick the wild garlic leaves that crowd the riverbank, and make soup.

I'm growing too—thinner, but taller. Today I'm

wearing an old green woollen skirt we found in the wardrobe, with the waistband turned over, and a big red jumper with the sleeves rolled back. We've kitted out Kelda with more clothes—some of my old ones and some from Grandma Frieda's wardrobe. We discovered a sewing basket, deep at the back of a cupboard, when we were playing hide-and-seek. Inside were spools of cotton thread in different colours, needles and buttons, and a pair of tiny scissors with handles shaped like a bird. I showed Kelda how to thread a needle, and how to sew big running stitches, so we could turn up the hems. I tried to remember how to knit with wool wound onto long knitting needles, like Nonna used to, but it's no good. I've forgotten, or maybe I never really knew.

Kelda comes dancing back, muddy and dishevelled. 'Let's get showered today!' she says. 'It's just about warm enough.'

'What do you mean?'

Kelda laughs. 'Under the waterfall. Rowan and me always wash, as soon as the summer comes.'

'It's hardly summer!' I say, but I'm excited too. How long since I've felt properly clean?

We bring two towels and the bar of ancient soap from the kitchen cupboard. Kelda leads the way, down the path, across the bridge, and up the other side to the flat rocks at the foot of the waterfall.

'This is where I saw the dipper bird,' I tell Kelda. There's no sign of it today. We're making too much noise.

Kelda chatters on. 'Not this rock. Not this one. We need to go higher, to the flat ledge where you can safely step right under the water. Come on! Higher.'

She isn't afraid, despite what happened to her before in the river. She's done this many times before with her brother; she likes showing me what to do. We undress and leave our clothes on the dry boulders next to the grass and edge towards the falling water.

Kelda is so thin and bony I can count each rib. Her hands and feet and legs are engrained with dirt. She is utterly unselfconscious. The girls at school were so obsessed with how they looked, they would never have dared do this.

'Skinny-dipping!' I say out loud. 'That's the name for this!'

Kelda laughs. ''Cos we're both skinny and we are like the dipper bird.'

She steps across the mossy boulders and plunges under the falling water. She gasps. She holds out her hand to me.

I take a deep breath and edge forward.

'AARGH!'

The water's ice-cold.

Kelda says something but it's impossible to hear anything above the roar and thunder of water. It tumbles over my head, streams over my body. I'm part of the waterfall now, I can't think or speak or do anything but gasp for breath. It's so cold it hurts; a million needles pummelling my skin.

Kelda shows me the hollowed rock behind the falling water, a ledge to sit on, half in and half out of the water. Sunlight catches the fine spray and makes tiny rainbows. I stay there as long as I can bear the cold, till I'm numb and frozen to the core.

I edge back along the slippery ledge. Kelda follows me.

Out of water and into air.

The blood sings along my veins. I feel joyous, totally alive.

We wrap ourselves in the towels and dance madly over the grass and laugh and laugh.

Kelda's lips are blue with cold, but her eyes are shining. I rub her wet hair for her, and bend down so she can do the same for me. We're shaky and shivery and the happiest we've been for ages.

'See? It was fun, wasn't it?' Kelda says through chattering teeth.

We get dressed slowly, our numb fingers fumbling, the clothes sticking to our damp skin. We run back to the house, and pile wood onto the kitchen stove to heat the kettle. We make nettle tea to warm us from the inside.

Early evening the same day, the first swallows arrive. Their twittering voices fill the sky. We watch them swoop and dive for flies in the fading light.

'How beautiful they are! It's a miracle, really. They've flown thousands of miles, across land and ocean and more land,' I tell Kelda. 'Wouldn't it be amazing if they were the exact same swallows I watched with Mamma and Dad!'

The chattering swallows fill me with new hope.

We made it! We're home!

'Rowan says they come back to the same nests where they were born,' Kelda says. 'There are nests in all the barns and under the eaves of the stone farmhouses. But how do they know the way? How do they find their nests again?'

'A sort of homing instinct. Or do they learn the way? Memorize it by landmarks, or smell, or something.'

Generations of swallows must have flown back to this house. The great-grandchildren of the swallows that Dad would have seen as a child, and they would have been the offspring of the swallows my grandmother would have seen, and her mother before that, a long line reaching back and back and back into the past.

'When will Rowan be home?' Kelda snuggles close. It's getting colder as daylight fades.

'Let's work it out. He left early yesterday.' I pick up two small stones and balance them on the wall. 'I guess that's time to cycle to the village schoolhouse, and stay a night. So, at least one more day to cycle back.'

Kelda picks up another stone.

The first stars appear. There are more stars here on a clear night than I have ever seen in my entire life. That's because there are no house lights, no street lights, for miles and miles and miles.

'Look! That's the North Star!' Kelda points. 'And there's the Plough. Those three stars are Orion's Belt.'

The stars make pictures, if you know how to look.

She's only seven, yet she knows these things because her brother has taught her, and because it matters if you live somewhere with no phone apps or maps. If you're lost at night, you need to know the way home. The stars are a compass. Perhaps the swallows follow the star pictures, too.

At bedtime, once Kelda's asleep, I open my sketchbook. Shadows from the flickering candle play across the blank page. I let my hand doodle swirls and lines with the coloured pencils. The swirls become swallows in a pale sky. I turn the page and fill the next spread almost entirely with dark grey and navy and black. I leave gaps for stars. Places for the light to shine through.

Make something beautiful.

A gift, for the future, the art shop man said.

Is that what we are doing, here? Making a new, beautiful life. Creating a future.

I pick up the pen he gave me. It's running out of ink.

Dear Marta,

I push on through tears.

Today was a good day.
We showered under a waterfall, and the swallows arrived.

Twenty-one

Kelda skips and dances ahead of me up the steep path. She's excited to be going to the barn at last.

Deep under the trees there are pools of blue where the bluebell flowers have opened out. Sunlight slants through the fresh green canopy. A cuckoo calls.

Kelda echoes back: *Cuckoo! Cuckoo!*

'Rowan might not be home yet, remember.'

She takes no notice of me. She's been unstoppable all morning, impatient to get moving.

We briefly rest at the ruined house, just enough for her to catch her breath and check for the fox. No sign. On we go.

'Kitty kitty kittens!' Kelda sings as she balances over

the rickety bridge, arms outstretched. 'I'm coming!'

Two buzzards circle silently in the pale blue sky above us. We follow the ridge path, over Swallow Fell and down the other side.

Kelda runs way ahead, slides down the muddy path, over the field and down to the barn.

Rowan's waiting at the door. He folds her into a massive hug.

'Well?' I say. 'Did you find anyone?'

'Yes.'

'And?'

'Three people. And a dog.'

'The three we saw?'

'Yes. Holly's the eldest, then Luke. Billy's about eight.'

'Brothers?'

'Holly's a girl. And Billy isn't their brother; they rescued him along the way. They've been moving about, not staying in any place for long. Survived the winter in the mine house, but they want to move on again soon.'

'Did you see the horrible dog?' Kelda asks.

'It's not horrible. Needs training, that's all. It's been let wild.'

'Where did they come from?' I ask.

'Further down the river valley. They're children like us. Ones who didn't get sick, and had to hide.'

So, I was right all along! But I don't say that to Rowan.

'Did you ask them about Dad?'

'Of course. They hadn't seen him. That shop has closed, though. The one he was heading for.'

'So, he had to search for another shop, another town. Maybe had to walk miles further. And that's why he's taking so long!'

'Maybe. If he's gone all the way to the coast,' Rowan says.

'I haven't given up, you know. He'll come home as soon as he can.'

Rowan nods.

'And if he doesn't, we will go and look for him. Or I will. I can borrow your bike.'

Kelda brings me one of the kittens to cuddle, but the kitten hates being held. It spits and scratches until I put it back down with the others.

'Were they friendly? Did you like them?' I ask Rowan.

He pauses.

Liking them or not isn't something he's thought about.

'I gave them a rabbit. We cooked and ate it together and talked a bit. I slept by their fire.'

'Talked about what?'

'The other places they've been. The villages all the way down the river are abandoned. No people. They've mostly been eating fish. They found a boat in a dilapidated boathouse downstream. Well, a canoe. One of those wide-bottomed wooden ones, big enough for the three of them and the dog.'

Kelda jumps up and down. 'When can I meet them? When? Tomorrow? It will be much better with people. Isabella's told me all about people. I want to go with you next time!' She repeats the names, sounding them out. 'Holly, Luke, Billy. Holly's my favourite.'

'You don't know that, silly!' Rowan says. 'You know nothing about her!'

'I like her name,' Kelda says. 'She sounds like us.'

Us? She means Rowan and her.

Rowan carries on. 'That day we saw them, they were looking for a shop or a farm with food. Didn't have a clue you were living in one of the houses. Or us, in the barn. They were shocked when I turned up.

'They're going to paddle upriver, when the water level goes down and the current isn't so strong. So you will meet them, Kelda.'

'Really?' Kelda's excitement spills over. She spins and dances round the table.

She stops next to the stove, suddenly serious.

'THAT's why it's so cold in here. The fire's gone out. You let the fire go out! What will we do now, Rowan? You said we must NEVER EVER let the fire go out!'

'I was away too long,' he says. 'I banked it up as best I could, but it went out anyway. And this morning I tried rubbing sticks together to make a spark, but I couldn't do it. Hopeless. And we don't have matches or a flint striker or anything like that.'

'How did you light it before?' I ask.

'We haven't ever let it go out. We've kept the fire alight all this time, ever since we ran out of matches.'

'There must be another way to make fire,' I say.

Kelda fusses over the kittens. Their eyes have changed from blue-grey to green-gold. They're playful and naughty and wild. The mother cat bats them with her paw when they are too annoying, chasing her tail and biting her ears. Rowan says they're still feeding from her, but she brings them other stuff to eat: mice and birds. 'She's teaching them to hunt.'

The tabby kitten is smaller and weaker than the others.

'It will probably die,' Rowan says. 'That's just nature. Survival of the fittest.'

'You're horrible,' Kelda says.

When he's not looking, she picks up the tabby kitten and tucks it under her jumper. She carries it like that all the way back to my house. Rowan and Kelda will stay with me tonight, till they can relight their fire.

Now we have a kitten to look after, too. We feed it scraps of raw rabbit and pigeon and fish: whatever we're going to cook for dinner. At night it's *supposed* to sleep in the kitchen next to the stove. The first night, Rowan tells Kelda she can't take it to bed with her, however much she pleads with him. 'You'll get fleas,' he says. 'You don't want fleas in your bed!'

'But it's just a baby. It will be scared and lonely all by itself.'

She calls the kitten Mouse, because it is so small.

The days pass.

Rowan and Kelda more or less move in with me. We don't discuss it. It's just simpler that way. Rowan seems not to mind. He's changing.

I guess it's more practical: three of us in one place, one fire to keep alight, one pile of logs to chop, one meal to cook, a proper house with a solid roof and walls and rooms. And maybe he's got used to it being the three of us. Maybe he likes me after all.

They go back and forth to the barn to check the cat and the other kittens, and to weed their vegetable garden and snare rabbits, but they come back each evening to sleep here. The hens and cockerel stay living here, too. We collect the eggs each day from all over the garden. We discover one broody hen sitting on a clutch of eggs under a giant rhubarb leaf in a wild, overgrown part of the garden, and we leave her there to sit till the chicks hatch. That way, we will have more chickens. More eggs.

We play hide-and-seek with Kelda because it's her favourite game. We find more hidden things in the house: a cardboard box with a board inside marked with numbered squares on it and pictures of snakes and ladders, and two dice to throw. We make up our own rules. We invent other games.

In the evenings we draw and make up stories. Rowan listens, but he doesn't join in. Sometimes he takes a book down from the shelf and leafs through the pages. Information books, mostly, about gardening and bees and plumbing. Big paper ordnance survey maps which he unfolds and studies and folds neatly away again.

We watch the swallows and house martins dipping and diving over the garden, catching insects. Sometimes the fox watches us from a safe distance, beyond the garden wall. 'It's biding its time,' Rowan says. 'Waiting for an opportunity.'

Every morning, Kelda goes down to the bridge to see the river. It's lower each day, now. Its voice is more a friendly conversation than a roar.

'They'll come soon, won't they? Holly and Billy and Luke. I'll be first to see them paddling under the bridge.'

Twenty-two

The back door bangs open and Kelda clatters into the kitchen. 'Rowan! Isabella!'

She runs into the dining room. 'There you are! I've seen them. The boat. They're almost here. Come on!'

Rowan and I follow her down the path towards the river.

Two teenagers and a younger boy with bare feet and rolled-up jeans are dragging a decrepit wooden canoe out of the river and up onto the bank. They tie it to a tree and put their socks and boots back on. They scramble up the bank to the path, muddy and exhausted but smiling, waving hello. 'Hi, Rowan!' the dark-haired boy calls.

Rowan waves back. 'That's Luke,' he says.

Kelda is already halfway down the bank to greet them.

'Where's your dog?' she calls.

'Jumped off, a way back. He'll soon catch up with us!' the girl says.

'I hope he's not chasing my fox.' Kelda makes her stern face.

'Just a squirrel,' the younger boy says. Billy. 'He won't catch it, he never catches anything. Don't worry. How come you have a fox?'

Kelda chatters to Billy as if they've been friends forever. It's like when she first met me. Non-stop questions. She tells him all about the barn, and falling in the river, and the fox.

It makes it easier for the rest of us.

I walk with Holly up to the house. She has cropped dark hair, and dark eyebrows and brown skin, and wears old combat trousers and a patched leather jacket and big boots. She's pretty cool. I ask her how old she is, and she says she thinks she's fifteen. 'It's hard to keep track of the months and years. Even the time of day,' she says. 'How do you do it?'

'We don't! There's daylight, and the times we're hungry, or really tired. That's all. Longer days, swallows and bluebells and cuckoos mean it's April here. But where I come from, in Italy, there are swallows all year round. I'm learning about everything. Anyway, it doesn't seem to matter so much about time. It's funny, 'cos back in the old life people went on about it *all the time.*'

'And now it's all about having enough to eat. Keeping warm. Being safe.'

'Was it dangerous,' I ask, 'paddling upstream?'

'More fun than dangerous. It hasn't rained for days and the river is quieter. It's hard work, though. And you get soaked. We take it in turns to paddle. Billy's not strong enough to keep going for long. It's a skill.'

'I'd like to learn,' I say.

She nods. 'I'll take you out, if you want.'

'We're here,' I say. 'This is my home.'

Holly stares up at the stone house.

I see it through her eyes: how solid and secure it must look compared to the ruined mine house Rowan described. 'My grandparents lived in it a long time ago,' I tell her. 'And my dad was brought up here. He's . . . not here at the moment. He went to get food and seeds. But he'll be back soon . . .' My voice peters out.

'Rowan told us.'

I nod.

'We had no idea anyone lived here. It was all shut up.'

'I was hiding. I was terrified. Thought you might be soldiers or police or horrible people who might hurt me . . .'

The dog bounds up the path, tail wagging, barking and bouncing up at Billy and Kelda.

Kelda backs away. 'You have to tie it up. I don't like it!'

Billy loops a piece of blue twine around its neck. 'He's just excited. Calm down, Finn.'

We go inside. Finn flops down under the kitchen table and rests his head on his shaggy paws.

Kelda eyes him warily. 'What sort is it?'

'A mix of lurcher and deerhound, we reckon,' Luke says.

The kitten watches the dog from a safe distance, perched on the top of a chair. She hisses when the dog moves a paw, or raises its head. The dog is massive and the kitten tiny, but it's obvious the kitten is going to be boss.

Rowan watches Holly like a hawk, the way he used to watch me when we first met.

We make stew with the fish Holly caught for us, a swap for Rowan's rabbit. We sit together around the kitchen table. Everyone's quiet as we eat. And then we begin to trade stories. How we came here. Where we're from. Plans.

Kelda's eyes widen as she listens. Her world is opening up, getting bigger. All she knew before was the barn, and the river and fells, the ruined house and the empty village. I've told her about a country called Italy, Europe, across the sea, and a different kind of life. Now we hear how Billy arrived in this country by boat from another place of war and destruction, and travelled north in a lorry, and lost his parents, probably to the sickness. He doesn't remember much about it. Holly and Luke found him on one of their explorations downriver, before winter floods made the lower reaches of the river impassable.

'Billy isn't his real name. He doesn't know what his real name was. We chose *Billy* together,' Holly says. 'It suits him.'

Holly was twelve and Luke nine when their mum got sick. She made them hide in the cellar when the men came to collect the sick and dying.

'We're all orphans. Except, it's just possible we might still have a dad somewhere,' Luke says. 'He never lived with us. So we don't know.'

'You can share my dad. He'll be back soon,' I say. 'And my mum, when she comes. And Gabriella. We can be a new kind of family. There's room enough in this house for everyone.'

Everyone goes a bit too quiet.

Holly and Luke glance at each other.

Rowan starts clearing the dishes.

'Well, just for tonight,' Holly says. 'Thanks, Isabella.'

Later, we light candles in the living room. I light the fire in there for the first time. Kelda shows Billy how to play the snakes and ladders game. She gives everyone a tour of the house. The only door we leave shut is Dad's room.

At dusk I go outside into the garden to shut the hens away. They go into the shed of their own accord these days, as soon as it gets dark. I count them. Five hens, and one angry cockerel.

The sixth hen is still sitting on her nest under the rhubarb leaves. I don't get too close.

She croons softly. Shifts her position on the eggs, fluffs her feathery chest over them to keep them warm. What if the fox comes tonight? She's so vulnerable. But Rowan says if we move the eggs she'll give up sitting, and the chicks inside the eggs will get cold and die. I go back to the shed and shoo the cockerel outside again, to keep watch for the fox.

I sit on the wall. The moon rises. The first stars appear. Voices from the house drift through the open back door. Laughter. Someone starts singing, and a second voice joins in. The house is full of people.

I've missed this so much: voices and laughter and song.

The piazza at dusk. The bells.

Antonia practising her scales on the flute.

Mamma calling Marta and me inside.

Twenty-three

Holly comes out to join me.

We sit in silence. Bats flit across the dark garden. An owl calls. The night garden is full of rustlings and creaks, and always there's the rushing river, louder in the dark.

Holly climbs up onto the wall and walks along it, arms out for balance. 'Is it amazing, living here? In a house which has been in your family for generations. Belonging somewhere.'

'I belonged in our city, at home. I've never thought much about this side of my family. It was a shock, coming here. Everything's so different.'

'It will all be different in your old city, now.'

'With the war, you mean?'

'Yes.'

'What have you heard?'

'Not much, but we saw people coming off a ship at the port. They'd had to leave everything. Run for their lives. Like Billy's mum and dad.'

I can't see her face in the dark. 'Where had the ship come from?'

'The Netherlands, I think. Or Belgium.'

'What will happen? How will it all end?'

'I don't know. The world's gone mad.'

She spins round, walks back to me along the wall, almost slips, regains her balance. 'Maybe it's people like us who will change things.'

'What do you mean?'

'Young people. People who can see new, better ways to live on our beautiful planet. Wasting nothing, not being greedy. You. Rowan and Kelda. Luke and Billy and me. Maybe we are the way forward. A blueprint for the future.'

'What's a blueprint?'

'A plan.'

'It wasn't by choice,' I say. 'It was forced on us.'

'Yes, but we're making it work, aren't we? OK, it's

been really hard. Cold, hungry, scared, sad, lonely; I know all that. But I'm more alive. Free. I'm weirdly happier now we have almost nothing.'

'I was happy before. I miss my family. Miss my friends. Miss my old home.'

A vixen calls from the fell: a wild, shrieking sound.

'The first time I heard that, I thought someone was being murdered!' I say.

'City girl!' Holly smiles.

'I guess I'm getting used to living here. Some days, it seems really beautiful. I see things differently. *I'm* different.'

My words surprise me. I hadn't known I was going to say that, but it's true. Life is much more clear and simple, reduced to what is essential.

'I'll take you out in the canoe tomorrow,' Holly says. 'Teach you how to paddle.'

The back door bangs open and Billy appears with the dog at his side. 'What're you two doing out here?'

'Nothing,' I say.

'Talking,' Holly says.

'You missed a game of snakes.'

'Fine by me. I've played it hundreds of times!' I say.

'Where are we all sleeping tonight?' Billy asks.

'Dog in the kitchen, you and Luke upstairs in the small bedroom at the side of the house,' Holly answers. 'I'll be on the sofa. I'll come and see you when you're in bed.'

She waits for Billy to go inside.

'Billy's had an even more horrible time than the rest of us,' she says. 'But he's getting better. He's stopped having nightmares. The dog helped. He loves that dog.'

'There's too much horribleness in the world.'

'Yes. So we focus on the good things instead. Every day. Even if they're tiny things.' She jumps down from the wall. 'I'm going in. Coming?'

'Not yet,' I say. 'Soon.'

I light two candles. I spread out the old paper maps on the big table in the dining room, so that they join up. I trace our river with my finger, from where it starts in the fells, then down a series of waterfalls, widening and deepening as it gets lower. I say the lovely place names out loud.

Stonesdale
Silver Wood

Green Gill
Black Hill
Duckingdub Bridge
Little Clumpstone
Winterings Edge

Rowan appears in the doorway. 'Talking to yourself?'

'Not really.'

I point to the name *Rowantree Hall* on the map. 'That should be your house!'

I show him how the road follows the river all the way to where it joins another river, and then down to the sea.

'There are hardly any towns the whole way. There's one at the coast, see? That must be where Dad's gone: all the way to the port. There will be shops there. A telephone line, even. And that's where Mamma and Gabriella will be arriving. They'll have travelled by bus or car, then got a boat across the North Sea. I expect he's waiting for them.'

Rowan sighs. 'It's possible, I guess.'

'Holly's been there. Seen the boats. People are definitely arriving that way from Europe. Anyway, you can see how far it is by road. Plus there are probably floods. Which explains why it's taking Dad so long. He would have sent a message to tell me if he could have, but there was no way to do that. He'll be terribly anxious about me.'

Rowan nods.

'But he needn't be. 'Cos I'm fine, really. I wish I could tell him. I hate to think of him being so worried. He'll be imagining me all alone and scared and hungry. He doesn't know about our garden, all the vegetables we're growing. The hens. You and Kelda. And now Holly, Luke, and Billy.'

'They'll be moving on,' Rowan says. 'They're not staying here. That's what they do: stay a while, move on.'

'But not yet. Don't spoil things. Let me be a little bit happy, Rowan.'

'Sorry.'

I hesitate. I want to tell him what Holly said, about us being the blueprint. But I don't want him to spoil that idea, either.

I fold the maps.

Rowan helps me.

'I really like her,' I say. 'Holly.'

He doesn't say anything.

I blow out one of the candles and take the other with me. 'Night, Rowan!'

The candle throws huge shadows up the stairs. Me, larger than life. A giant Isabella, climbing upstairs.

Twenty-four

We untie the canoe and push it gently down the bank to the river. Holly climbs in first. She holds the canoe steady with her paddle and I clamber in too, much less gracefully. It wobbles. I grab the sides.

She laughs. 'Sit down.'

It's early morning. Mist hangs like breath over the water.

'We'll go downstream, while you're learning,' she says. 'When you feel balanced, start paddling. Just do what I do.'

She dips her paddle one side then the other, holds it still against the water near the bow, and twists it to alter the direction of the canoe. She makes it look easy, but I know it isn't. We went on kayaks on the river as a school trip once. They made us practise safety drills: lining up all the kayaks to keep everyone stable when the big boats powered upriver, and how to capsize and right the kayak by yourself with a twist of your body. Except, Marta and I got the giggles, and ended up swimming, the kayak drifting away downriver. We had to be rescued by the instructor.

This is a different kind of canoe, made of wood, not fibreglass, broader and more stable. I pick up the second paddle, dip one side, then the other, copying Holly. Drops of river water bead along the wooden paddle, catch the sunlight and turn to gold. My arms soon ache, but I keep paddling.

The canoe glides on the smooth, brown river through a tunnel of trees. The banks are alive with insects and small creatures, voles or mice. Moorhens and coots dabble in the shallows. Holly steers us between rocky boulders, closer to the bank where the current isn't so strong. 'Duck!' she shouts, as we sweep under low-hanging branches. 'Hazel and alder trees,' she says. 'We practically lived on hazelnuts last autumn.'

Shafts of sunlight sift through the trees and make liquid green and gold patterns on the water. Where the river widens, swallows and martins fly low enough to scoop up water to drink. Midges hang in columns in the shady, slower edges of the river. The river gurgles and sucks and babbles and sings.

Something tiny and brilliant blue flashes across the water.

'Kingfisher!' Holly says.

We rest the paddles for a moment but the river won't let us stay still. It tugs and pushes the canoe onward.

'We'll tie up so you can have a rest,' Holly yells above the sound of the water. She paddles us towards the bank and grabs a bunch of rushes to pull us closer. She pushes the paddle down to the riverbed to hold the canoe still. There's a sudden stink of mud and river silt.

The canoe bobs gently under the tall weeds on the bank: nettles and dock, wild clematis, twisted willow. Bees and flies hum in the thick vegetation.

'Wow! That was amazing!' I can't stop smiling.

'You got the hang of it pretty quick. But it makes your arms ache, yes?'

'Yes.'

'And it will be harder going back upstream.'

'I'm much stronger than I used to be,' I say.

'We should have brought something to eat,' Holly says. 'I'm starving.'

'Where are we?'

'No idea.'

Everything looks different from river level. But we've not passed under any bridges, so we can't have gone far. Above the river bank there's a grass field and beyond that a glimpse of bracken and heather-covered fell. Blue sky.

'Next time, I'll show you how we catch fish. OK, ready to go back?'

'Yes.'

'We'll swap seats, so you can be in front this time.' Holly stands up, and balances the canoe while I shift forward.

I pick up my paddle.

We set off.

Holly shouts instructions from the back of the canoe. 'Look out! Left a bit!'

It's hard to hear her above the rush of the water. The river runs shallow over stones in some places, and in others, there are boulders that must have been washed down from the fells in winter floods over the years. If we scrape against them they'll make holes in the wooden skin of the canoe.

In the deeper middle of the river the current is stronger. My arms ache from paddling hard against the flow. We can't rest for a second because the river simply carries the boat back. It takes twice, maybe three times as long to travel up to our bridge.

Kelda and Billy are hanging over the bridge. They wave as we come into view. We paddle out of the main flow, into the shallows under the trees.

'We thought you'd both run away!' Kelda calls down.

Billy slides down the muddy bank to help us tie up. He hugs Holly and she ruffles his hair. 'No such luck!' she tells him. 'You've got me for life.'

He takes one paddle and I bring the other. My legs are shaky.

'Does it leak?' Kelda asks.

'No, but water splashes from the paddles. I'm soaked!'

Kelda and Billy run ahead, back to the house. The

dog barks as we get closer. They've left him tied up in the garden.

'Rowan said you'll be moving on soon,' I say to Holly. 'Where will you go?'

'West and north. Over the moor and the high fells to the other side. Out of this valley. We've explored the whole length of it now.'

'Aren't you scared of being seen?'

'Not any more.'

'Rowan's still obsessed about staying hidden.'

'The sickness was nearly three years ago. Life moves on. Things change. We need to find out what's happening in other places.' She looks at me. 'Do you want to come with us?'

Do I? A part of me does. Being friends with Holly, exploring new places . . . But not yet.

'I need to be here, for when Dad and Mamma and Gabriella arrive.'

'Oh. Yes. Of course.'

'Come back and visit,' I say. 'Let us know what you find.'

She nods. 'We won't be able to carry the canoe over the hills. We'll leave it here, for you. Might be useful. Fishing. Transport. Yes?'

'Really? You're sure?'

'We'll come back for it if we need it, so keep it safe.'

'Yes.'

'You did pretty well, paddling. You'll be safe enough. Can you swim? Can Kelda and Rowan?'

'I can. I don't think Kelda has ever learned. But I can teach her. She needs to learn.'

I tell Holly about her falling in the river. How she nearly died.

'We're all survivors, one way and another,' she says.

'Survival of the fittest, Rowan calls it. Like animals, and plants. Evolution.'

She laughs. 'Maybe we are a new species that's evolved. *Evolving.*'

'The Children of Swallow Fell. Children of the future.'

'Where's Rowan?' I ask Kelda.

'Gone to the barn with Luke.' She wanders off, following the hens around the wild garden.

Billy, Holly, and I are weeding the vegetable garden, watering the beans and peas and potatoes.

'That's the thing about moving on all the time,'

Holly says. 'You can't make a garden. No time to grow things.' She laughs. 'We're the hunter-gatherers; you and Rowan and Kelda are the first settlers.'

'Eh?' Billy says.

'That's how civilizations started. Nomads and hunter-gatherers first—wandering folk, hunting wild animals and gathering nuts and berries and edible plants. That's a bit like us. Then people stopped moving around, settled near water, grew crops, made homes. Kept animals. A bit like Isabella and Rowan.'

Kelda dances over. 'The eggs have hatched! There are five tiny chicks! Come and see!'

Tiny balls of fluff scuttle around the mother hen. She fusses and croons and clucks. They're brand new, but already they are learning to fend for themselves. The mother hen shows them how to peck and scratch for food.

A big black crow flies over the garden and the chicks run to hide under their mother's feathery body until danger has passed.

'How do they know it means danger?' I ask.

'Instinct, I guess. Built in.'

The cockerel crows from his perch on the low wall.

'Did you hear him this morning? So early!'

Kelda and Billy bring five new-laid eggs they've collected from the wild garden.

For lunch, we have omelettes with garden herbs and dandelion leaf salad.

'What food do you most miss?' Holly asks.

'Lasagne. And chips!' I say. 'And ice cream.'

'Lemon pie.' Billy.

'Curry and rice.' Holly.

Kelda doesn't miss anything. She can't, because she's too young to remember the time *before*.

We put the garden tools back in the shed. Holly looks around, sees the piles of rope, the logs. 'Let's make a swing for Kelda.'

We knot the shorter bits of rope together. Holly's good at the knots. She shows me how to tie a reef knot. We find a flattish log big enough to make a seat, and drill holes to thread the ropes through. It takes ages.

'Which tree shall we use?'

'Not the apple tree, because of the nests.'

In the end we choose the old rowan tree in the field at the side of the house. Holly pulls herself up the tree, climbs higher, ties the ropes over a strong branch. 'Now try swinging!' she calls down to me.

The seat is low to the ground. I hold the ropes tight in either hand, check they hold my weight, and then I begin to swing. It's a movement so familiar, a memory in my body from when I was little: push off, lean backwards, lean forwards. Stretch out my legs, push back and forward with my whole body.

I go higher and higher on the long ropes: steady, slow, beautiful arcs. The air rushes past my face. It's exhilarating, the closest thing to flying.

Holly laughs from high in the tree. 'Hold on tight!'

I stop pushing and let the swing slow down until I'm back to earth.

'Wow! That was magical!'

Holly clambers down and jumps from the lowest branch. 'My turn!'

Now Billy and Kelda have come to watch.

They try swinging together, with Holly and me pushing them. They get the hang of it; they learn how to swing higher by themselves.

'We should have made a swing before.'

'Yeah. You can't be working all the time! You need to have fun, too.'

'Kelda's always playing. Hide-and-seek, endlessly! Make-believe games. Stories. She makes me and Rowan join in.'

'Billy doesn't. We forget how young he is.' Holly looks at me. 'Want to go out in the canoe again? This time we'll fish.'

We paddle downstream like the last time, and stop in a deep, shady spot. Midges dance above the water. Birds call from deep in the tangle of trees and bushes on the riverbank. The river current flows swiftly as it sweeps close to the opposite bank on the bend in the river, but here the water is still and dark.

'Perfect,' Holly whispers. She takes a dried-out worm from a tin and spears it on a hook on the end of a line of string, and she dangles it over the edge of the canoe, down into the depths. We wait.

The air smells of wild garlic, and mud, and the dank watery river smell. The canoe rocks when either of us moves. We try to stay still and patient. Further downriver, two small dippers bob from stone to stone, dive right under the water, and appear again. The birds, the light on the water, the dark shadows, the shapes and colours—I try to hold it all in my mind, so I can draw it later.

The string wiggles, jerks, and tightens, and Holly braces herself against the side as she pulls up the string and lands a small brown flapping, gasping trout. She unhooks its mouth and whacks it sharply against the canoe to put it out of its misery.

Sudden death.

'Sorry, fish,' I say.

Holly rolls her eyes. 'Too soft, that's what you are.'

'Rowan says that, too. But the rabbits . . . especially the little ones. Urgh!'

'Imagine having to kill and butcher a deer. Or a goat. Or something even bigger.'

'No thanks.'

'But you can manage a fish. Practise with the next one.'

'Fish have feelings too, you know. Even worms, probably.'

'Well, OK. But we have to eat something. Can't survive on a handful of leaves.'

I put a worm on the bent hook. Cast the homemade line. Wait.

Finally I feel the tug and twist of the string. Gently

pull up the line; a small speckled trout thrashes and gasps on the hook. Whack it dead.

Repeat. Repeat. Repeat.

It gets a bit easier each time.

We have to eat to survive. We won't waste anything. We won't take more than we need. Sorry, sorry, sorry.

Supper is a feast. We cook the fish with garlic leaves. Luke and Rowan make a tasty rabbit stew. Tonight there's enough for us all to eat until our bellies are full and satisfied. It's a celebration: new friends, new world.

We take turns on the swing. Finn the dog runs round and round the field and Kelda and Billy try to teach him to come, to chase sticks and bring them back, to sit and stay.

Finn won't do as he's told. He bounds over the rough grass, chases imaginary prey, barks at the birds.

'He wants his freedom, same as us,' Holly says.

The light fades, shadows deepen; we traipse back to the garden. We put the hens to bed in the shed. The five new chicks scurry in after their mother.

Together we build a bonfire in the wild part of

the garden, and sit around it to watch the swallows. Luke stirs the fire to send sparks spiralling upwards. Kelda and I bring out blankets for everyone, to wrap around us as the sun goes down and the air chills. Finn curls up next to Billy. Everyone's sleepy.

'We'll be leaving early in the morning,' Holly says.

'You'll come back and tell us what you find?'

'Yes. You'll keep the canoe safe?'

'Yes.'

I wish there was something I could give Holly, to remember me by.

The fire dies down to embers. We stay around it, wanting this moment to last and last, the six of us bound together by the new lives we're creating for ourselves in this hidden valley.

Night falls. Stars blaze in the heavens. The river rushes on.

Twenty-five

It's still dark, but the cockerel has crowed and so it must be nearly morning. Someone's moving around downstairs—Holly, getting ready to leave. They have hardly any stuff to carry—a bag for food and water bottles, a change of clothes. I get dressed quickly and go downstairs.

'I wish you weren't going,' I blurt out.

Holly doesn't say anything.

'It's OK, I know you have to. But even so . . .' I blather on.

'You'll be fine,' she says.

'I'll miss you!'

'Anyway, you might move on too.'

'Maybe.'

'With your family, when they arrive. Who knows? Or the war will end, and you can go back to your old home. Is that what you want?'

'I don't know. Yes, if it's safe, I suppose. But then I'd have to leave Rowan and Kelda behind.'

'Complicated, yes. And going *back* isn't always the right thing to do.'

'Can I . . . would you . . . There's something I wondered . . .'

'What?'

'Letters. A bundle of letters. Would you take them for me? Maybe post them, when you get somewhere where that's possible.'

'What kind of letters?'

'My letters to Marta. My best friend back home.'

'OK,' Holly says. 'Go and get them. If you're sure.'

The letters are neatly stacked in the bottom drawer in the chest in my room. I kneel on the floor and lift them out. Eighteen altogether, some short, others over several pages. I bundle them together and take them downstairs.

'Are there too many? Can you fit them in your bag?'

'Yes.'

'She must be a very special friend, your Marta.'

'She is. She's been my best friend since we were babies. We saw each other every day. We went to the same schools. We spoke every evening. She stayed at our flat all the time. We were like twins . . .

'And . . . that day, when the war came . . . we said goodbye on our way home from school, and . . . and that's when the explosion happened at the tram station, when the bombs started . . . and Marta was on her way to the tram station at that exact same time. And after that, her phone didn't work. And then the next day we had to leave on the train, and I left without knowing what happened to Marta . . . Except I do know, really.' I start to weep. And now I've started I can't stop.

I shall never see Marta again.

Holly just stays close, not saying anything.

She hugs me briefly, but she's not really a hugging person.

She waits while I sniff and blow my nose and wipe my face.

She hands me back the parcel of letters. 'I don't think I should take these, Isabella.'

I nod.

'Keep them safe till you're really ready to let them go. Then do something beautiful with them. Burn them in a bright bonfire, or set them sailing down the river, or something else lovely.'

I can't speak. My heart's too full. But I know she's right.

I take the letters upstairs, and tuck them safely in the drawer, and I walk slowly back downstairs again.

I help Holly fill the water bottles from our spring. She goes to wake Billy and Luke.

The garden is cool, dewy. A blackbird sings from the top of the apple tree. Mist hangs along the river. I gulp deep breaths of the cold air and gradually my heart steadies and my head clears.

The fox runs up the steep slope of the fell, a streak of red against the bright green grass. A snail leaves a silvery trail over the dug earth. The sky is clearing to blue, the wisps of cloud disappearing as the sun gets stronger. It's the perfect morning for their long walk.

We watch them go, Kelda and Rowan and me. We don't speak. The dog runs ahead of them, back and forth. They climb the hill, up and up. They stop and wave at us, and then on they go. Three figures silhouetted against the light.

It keeps happening. People leave. Loss after loss.

The house and the garden are too quiet and empty.

Rowan says he's going to the barn. Luke's given him a flint striker for lighting the fire.

Kelda walks down to the field and sits on the swing, and rocks back and forth, feet on the ground. She begins to swing properly, higher and stronger.

I call to her. 'I'm going up to the ruined house. Want to come?'

She jumps off the swing and runs across the field, skirt flapping.

She slips her hand into mine.

'We'll take Mouse with us,' she says, 'to visit her mother and brothers at the barn, yes?'

'Maybe you should leave her at the barn,' I say. 'She must be missing them.'

Kelda runs back to the house, and comes back with the kitten in her arms. It mews, and flexes tiny needle claws. She tucks it close under her jumper.

The raven takes off from the roof as we arrive. It flaps slowly in a direct line to the other side of the river valley. 'Imagine being able to do that!' I say.

Kelda flaps one arm, an imaginary wing. She has to hold the kitten tight with the other.

'This is where I first met you!' I say.

Kelda puts the kitten down inside the ruined house. It crouches low, and creeps forward cautiously to sniff and explore this new place.

'I don't know why I keep coming here. It's as if the house calls me.'

Kelda laughs. 'How can a house do that? That's daft!'

'I know. But that's how it is.'

It would have been a lovely house, once upon a time. I screw up my eyes and imagine the stone walls and slate roof solid and new, glass in the windows, a front door, furniture, a fire in the hearth, a family with lots of children running about.

'It's a happy house!' Kelda says, suddenly. 'That's why you like it.'

'Yes!'

'Once upon a time a girl called Alice lived here. She had a pet fox and a sheepdog puppy, and a white cat. People called her a *wild child* because she ran free and didn't go to school and did whatever she wanted.'

'Like you!'

'Maybe *my* fox is a little bit tame because her great-great-grandmother was Alice's tame one.'

'That's a nice thought.' I smile at Kelda. 'Or maybe it's because you give it food! I'm not sure you can really have a *pet* fox. A fox is a wild animal. It needs to be wild to survive.'

Kelda scoops up the kitten. It purrs, a tiny, tentative purr, still learning how to do it. 'Shall we go on to the barn now?'

'You can. I want to stay here a bit longer.'

Did I know? How could I have known?

I sit for ages looking out over the valley.

Everything is brilliantly vivid to me.

Wind ripples through the patches of bracken and grass and heather on the high moorland, turning it alive: the soft pelt of a breathing animal. There's the constant trickling of water: small streams tumbling down the fell in rills and pools and falls to the river in the valley bottom. A pair of silent buzzards circle high above the wooded edge of the fell: oak, birch, rowan, hawthorn, ash. Tight white flower buds on the dark twigs of hawthorn. Sphagnum moss like carpets of green stars.

How could I have ever thought this place empty and desolate, nowhere and nothing!

It takes a moment to register the new sound in the valley.

A car. Coming slowly up the valley road.

The engine wheezes as it changes down a gear, bumps over potholes, splashes through the ford. The car comes into view: small and blue, a bit battered. Too far off to actually see who's driving, but who else could it possibly be? No one comes here.

I know it's Dad.

I'm already running back home to greet him.

Twenty-six

The car's parked in front of the house. The front door's wide open, and Dad's standing there.

'Dad!'

'Isabella!'

We run to each other and we hug and hug and words spill out but make no sense at first. We gabble, and talk over each other. We stop talking altogether, and we laugh and we cry some more.

'You're safe!' he says. 'You're OK! I've been frantic!'

'I wished I could let you know I was all right. More than all right! There's so much to tell you ...' I hug him again. 'And Mamma and Gabriella ...?'

'OK. Safe. I finally got through to Mum. They're slowly making their way over. They'll get one of the boats across. Mum sends you all her love. They've had a hard time. Horrible.'

My words tumble out. About Rowan and Kelda. Holly, Luke, and Billy. 'They've only just left,' I say. 'They'll keep moving on. They might come back for the canoe, and tell us what they've found. But you can meet Rowan and Kelda very soon!'

'Good!' Dad says.

I show him the swing, the wood store, the garden.

'Rowan snares rabbits and pigeons. He's taught me which wild plants we can eat. Come and see what we're growing.'

'You're amazing!' Dad keeps saying. 'Amazing. Creating all this!'

'Not just me. Rowan and Kelda and me, together.'

He watches the hens. 'Mam kept chickens when I was a child.' He smiles.

I make us real tea with teabags. It tastes weird, too bitter after Rowan's nettle and heather teas.

We sit at the kitchen table and little by little, Dad tells me the story of his long journey to the coast, his search for a shop selling food, for a phone that worked. How he got ill, and had to stay away even longer. How terrible he felt that there was no way to let me know. 'I was desperate, worrying about you,' he says.

'Are things really bad, back home?'

'Yes,' he says. He doesn't want to tell me how bad it really is. 'People have lost their lives. People we know.'

He stands with his hands in his pockets and looks out at the garden and the fells beyond. 'This place is a haven of peace and sanity, Isabella. You've no idea.'

He doesn't mention Marta. I don't need to ask. Deep down, I already know.

The rest of the day, Dad keeps staring at me.

'What?'

'You look different. Older!'

I show him my drawings in the sketchbook. He leafs through the pages. He loves the paintings that Kelda and I have been doing. Our drawings. One thing per day: a picture diary.

'We used up most of your paints and pens,' I tell him. 'Sorry.'

'I'm glad,' he says. 'These are beautiful, Isabella.'

'Kelda's learning to read. She's never had books of her own.'

'When can I meet her?'

'She and Rowan will have heard the car. They'll be hiding in their barn. I'll go and fetch them. I'll tell them it's you, and it's safe for them to come. Rowan will be suspicious at first. But that's just how he's had to be.'

There's so much more to tell Dad. The sickness. Rowan's fear they'd be taken away. Kelda falling in the river, and me looking after her . . .

Dad listens, tears in his eyes.

Everything changes, that's what Holly said. *It's the one thing you can be sure of.*

It's evening. We sit at the kitchen table: Dad, Rowan, Kelda, and me.

Kelda leans forward to see what Dad's drawing. The kitten purrs on her lap. She feeds it tiny pieces of the fish we're cooking.

'It's Mouse!' she says. 'It's really good. Do another one! Draw me!'

Dad's happy, like he used to be when I was Kelda's age and he drew pictures for me.

Dinner's ready. Rowan serves the fish stew. I take the flatbreads from the pan on the stove and place them on the table.

Kelda helps herself. 'Delicious!'

'Thank you,' Dad says. 'Thank you for this, and for everything.' He closes his eyes, murmurs words: the blessing that Nonna used to say at family mealtimes.

He looks at us, sitting together around the table, and tears come into his eyes again.

'The best meal I've had my entire life,' he says.

'Later, we'll have fresh peas and broad beans,' Rowan says. 'Potatoes, in the summer.' He's still watching Dad the whole time. Doesn't dare trust him, yet, but he's gradually getting used to him being here.

Kelda chatters on. She tells Dad about the waterfall shower, and Holly's canoe, and the river, like a song.

'We used to make paper boats, when I was a child,' he tells her. 'We'd sail them on the river.'

'Show me how!' Kelda says, but she's already yawning.

'Tomorrow,' Dad says.

We make our paper boats after breakfast.

Dad helps Kelda fold the paper. She writes a big letter K for Kelda on the side.

She hops up and down. 'Come on, hurry up, Isabella!'

'I'll be there in a moment,' I say. 'Just need to get something from upstairs.'

She runs down to the bridge where Rowan and Dad are waiting.

The morning mist is already thinning; the river dances with light.

We launch the boats from the riverbank, gently pushing them away to set them sailing.

'Close your eyes and make a wish!' I say.

The boats float off together, swirling and bobbing on the water.

They speed up, swept along in the flow of the river, under the shadow of trees, into the darkness and out again, back into sunlight.

Seven boats, each marked with a letter.

I and K and R, D for Dad and G for Gabriella and M for Mum.

And one more with a letter M, for Marta.

'Coming back to the house?' Dad says.

'Not yet,' I say. 'There's something I need to do first. By myself.'

'OK,' Dad says.

Kelda and Rowan walk back with him.

I wait on the river bridge till they're out of sight. I listen to the voice of the river, and the wind in the trees like breath.

A kingfisher flies across the water, a dart of brilliant turquoise.

When you're ready, Holly said.

I'm ready, now.

I pull the bundle of letters from my pocket. I don't read them again. I did that last night, alone in my bedroom.

I tear each page into tiny pieces.

Letter by letter, I let them go.

Goodbye, Marta.

The paper pieces flutter down from the bridge. They float for a few seconds and are swept away in the flow of the river, whirled downstream and out of sight.

A few of the pieces stay floating for longer, white paper moths on the water.

The last fragments sink and disappear.

My letters to Marta are part of the river now, along with the silt and stones and the peat-gold water and the bubbles of air and light: new notes in the river's song.

And Marta will always be a part of me.

Postscript

When war came, it came swiftly and suddenly, right into the heart of our lives. It changed everything.

But we made a new life, in a new place.

We started all over again.

Rowan, Kelda, and me: Isabella.

Dad, Mamma, and Gabriella.

This is our life now.

On sunny days we swim in the river, or paddle downstream in Holly's canoe. We swing under the tree. We work in the garden, tend the vegetables, weed and plant and harvest our food. Catch fish, snare rabbits, pick wild berries. Dry wild heather flowers to make tea. Sit outside under the stars. Talk and laugh and sing and tell each other stories.

The world keeps on turning.

When the days get shorter again we'll hunker down for autumn. Live off nuts and berries, wild mushrooms, rabbit stew, and fish. Chop wood for the stove. Draw and paint and write. Have our last showers under the waterfall, before winter dark and ice set in.

Our life. It's a free and happy life, a simple life, taking only what we need. Caring for each other. Sharing what we have. Helping and healing.

A life for a future.

Acknowledgements

Thank you to my editors Liz Cross
and Clare Whitston, my agent Jodie Hodges,
to Helen Crawford-White for her wonderful
cover image, and to the team at
Oxford University Press.

About the author

Julia Green has written 19 books for young people.
She writes about the relationship between children and the
natural world, islands and oceans, friendship, family, love, loss,
and adventure. Julia was born in Ashtead, Surrey; currently she
lives in Bath but spends as much time as she can in wild, remote
places. She loves the hilltops, woodlands, the sea, beaches, and
islands. She has two adventurous grown-up sons.

Julia founded the renowned MA Writing for Young People
at Bath Spa University which has launched the careers of
many children's writers. She is Emeritus Professor in Writing
for Young People. She enjoys leading creative writing
workshops for children and adults in a variety of settings,
including festivals and schools.

You can find out more about Julia on her website
www.julia-green.co.uk

Follow her on Twitter **@JGreenAuthor**

Visit her author page on Facebook **@JuliaGreenAuthor**

Also by Julia Green

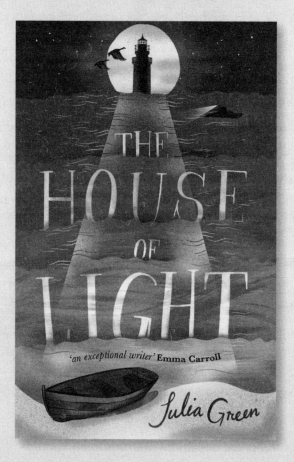

'an exceptional writer' Emma Carroll

Julia Green

It's always just been Bonnie and Granda,
living off the land, keeping to themselves and
out of trouble. Until one day, Bonnie goes
scavenging on the beach and finds a battered
rowing boat, and a bare-footed boy. He's cold,
hungry, and in need of shelter. Bonnie knows it's a
crime to help this stranger boy, but she can't leave
him for the border guards to find.

The longer she cares for this boy, who has
travelled across oceans for a new beginning,
the more Bonnie longs for her own freedom.
Perhaps it's time to escape the life she's always
known, to move out of the darkness, and set
sail for the house of light . . .

Also by Julia Green

JULIA GREEN

To the Edge of the World

A new life. A fearless friend. A wild sea adventure . . .

Jamie lives on an island out west—a wild place
of wind, waves, and surging tides. He loves
the island, but fears the surrounding ocean.

Mara lives on the island too—she's fearless.
The only thing that worries her is being sent away
to school. When that threat becomes too real,
she knows it is time to plan her escape.

And that's when Jamie, Mara, and her
dog Django find themselves swept away on
a wild sea adventure beyond anything they
have dreamed of . . .

Ready for more great stories? Try one of these...

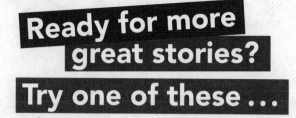

THE **SOUP** MOVEMENT

★ BEN DAVIS ★

A HUMOROUS AND HEART-WARMING TALE, INSPIRED BY A TRUE STORY

ALI SPARKES

NIGHT FOREVER

SCARED OF HEIGHTS? THAT'S THE LEAST OF YOUR PROBLEMS.

CERRIE BURNELL

The Ice Bear Miracle

JOE WILSON

THE ISLAND THAT DIDN'T EXIST